I0573401

Dames are his hobby
but his business is
DEATH

Peter Chambers finds out the hard way that a private eye should never sign on for more than his fair share of corpses—or dames.

Take this particular case.

For Chambers it starts out like the realization of every man's dream. With a half dozen or so luscious lovelies from the cast of the hit musical *Flesh and Fury* vying for his favors. It swings into action with a sizzling European movie siren calling his name.

And then it turns into a nightmare. One by one Chambers meets a heel, a hood, a hellion. Three very different people who share one common

kick: **MURDER.**

Fistful of Death

Henry Kane

PROLOGUE BOOKS

F+W Media, Inc.

Published in electronic format by
PROLOGUE BOOKS
an imprint of F+W Media, Inc.
10151 Carver Road
Blue Ash, Ohio 45242
www.prologuebooks.com

Copyright © 1958 by Henry Kane

All rights reserved.
No part of this publication may be reproduced or transmitted in any form or
by any means, electronic or mechanical, including photocopy, recording, or any
information storage or retrieval system, without permission in writing from the
publisher.

eISBN 10: 1-4405-3909-X
eISBN 13: 978-1-4405-3909-1

POD ISBN 10: 1-4405-5788-8
POD ISBN 13: 978-1-4405-5788-0

This is a work of fiction. Names, characters, corporations, institutions,
organizations, events, or locales in this novel are either the product of the author's
imagination or, if real, used fictitiously. The resemblance of any character to actual
persons (living or dead) is entirely coincidental.

This work has been previously published in print format by:
Signet Books, The New American Library, New York, NY.

ONE

THE OLD MAN was as unlikely as hominy grits at El Morocco. Or should I say crêpes suzette at Nedicks? Or is it Eggs Benedict at Bertha's Beanery? First off, although he said he was sixty-two, he looked no more than forty-two, with a tall trim figure, a deeply tanned face—although this was November—and a handshake with more firm squeeze than a double-barreled blackmailer fresh off a whisper magazine. Secondly, he was a banker who was throwing away a thousand dollars, and bankers who throw away money are as unlikely as ungarnished meatballs at La Chambord. Thirdly, he had popped into the office without previous call or appointment, and business men who pop into business offices without previous call or appointment are as unlikely as feature spreads of gefilte fish on the snazzy menus of Royal House on Fifty-seventh and Park.

"What brought you here in the first place?" I said.

"I was recommended," he said, "by Agatha Levine."

Agatha Levine was an actors' agent, and a good one.

"When was this?" I said.

"About fifteen minutes ago." He slumped lower in the customer's chair, stretched his long legs and crossed his ankles. "I came here directly from her office."

His name was Edward Duff. He was senior partner of the banking firm of Duff, Sherman and Becker, principal offices in the salutary city of Beverly Hills in the golden State of California.

"What's the connection," I said, "between you and Agatha Levine?"

"She's an old and trusted friend," he said.

I ceased and desisted, momentarily, from further questioning. I was ready for remonstrance, but remonstrance, if I may be forgiven, was slightly premature. Temptation, in the form of ten crisp bills in the sum total of a thousand dollars, lay spread on my desk. I cast a covertly covetous glance at temptation; then I seized temptation by the horns, if hundred dollar bills can be said to have horns. I reached out and gathered temptation into a neat green packet and stuffed it out of sight into my desk drawer. I sighed and I said:

"Why do you insist upon throwing your money away?"

"Because I think it's a solid investment."

"But she's due back tomorrow, isn't she?"

"That's right."

"Due back from where, Mr. Duff?"

"I don't know."

That held me for a moment. I moved lower in my chair and now, across the desk, I was looking at him eye to eye. "You don't know where she is, Mr. Duff?"

"That's it exactly, Mr. Chambers."

"But you do know she's due tomorrow?"

"Yes, Mr. Chambers."

"Then why don't you wait until tomorrow—and ask her?"

"Because there's more to it than that, if you please."

"I please," I said.

"As long as I've had the impulse to take this step, I'd like to go all the way."

"What's all the way?" I said.

"I'd like a complete report. I suppose, in a way, it's sneaky—"

"A father checking on his daughter?"

"Sneaky, don't you think?"

"Yes," I said. "I think."

"But the circumstances are rather unusual."

"I'll know that," I said, "when you acquaint me with said circumstances." But I was beginning to feel better about temptation in my desk drawer. "Where do you want to begin, Mr. Duff?"

"At the beginning, naturally."

"Naturally," I said.

"I'm a widower," he said.

"Sorry," I said.

"I have two children, two daughters."

"Yes?" I said, sitting up, snatching at a pencil, real business-like, poised for making notes on a pad of yellow paper. "Yes?" I said.

"Vivian, she's the older one."

"How old?"

"Twenty-five, married, and with two children of her own." I made my notes. "And your other child?"

"Katy. She'll be eighteen five months from now. We all live together on the West Coast in a big old house in Bel-Air." He sat up, lit a cigarette, inhaled deeply. "Vivian and Katy," he said. "Different as day and night."

"Which one would you say was night?"

"Katy. Kind of a hellion. Always was. Oh, a good kid, down deep inside of her, but the kind of a kid who could go either way, if you know what I mean."

"I can't say I do, exactly."

"Are you married, Mr. Chambers?"

"No, I'm not," I said.

6

"Then of course you can't say." He squinted thoughtfully. "Now how shall I put it?" He shuffled in the chair, uncomfortably, still squinting, seeming to be trying to select the right words for what he had to say. "Bringing up kids, in these times, in this day and age, it's rough, real rough, rougher than you, as a bachelor, can imagine."

"Hasn't it always been rough? I mean—"

"Always a problem, of course, but not as much of a problem as . . . today." He puffed hard on the cigarette, wiped it out in the ashtray. The lines on his long lean face appeared deeper. "Essentially, our kids are post war products, brought up in an era when guns, knives, violence are commonplace matters. The . . . the entire aura of our times is one of violence, the entire climate one of insecurity. The hot war and its backwash, the cold war and its threat, the bombs of utter destruction, the intercontinental missiles . . ." He brought out a new cigarette. "Sorry," he said, "if I kind of let myself go, but it does have application."

"To Katy?"

"To all kids, Katy included. You've just got to be lucky!"

"Yeah, I suppose," I said.

"I was lucky with Vivian. She was a plain, sweet, fine girl who grew up to be a plain, sweet, fine woman. Not so Katy. I just wasn't that lucky with Katy. I'm trying to explain a good deal in a short time, Mr. Chambers. Please bear with me."

"I'm bearing," I said.

"To begin with, Katy was always beautiful, very very beautiful."

"That's a complaint?" I said.

"Not a complaint, but a complication. A beautiful girl is always admired, always the center of attraction. That doesn't help, in the growing-up stage. Plus she was always big for her age."

"What's that got to do with it, Mr. Duff?"

"It relates, it all relates to my being here right now."

"Her being big for her age?"

"She ran around with older boys. Why, at fourteen, she looked—practically nineteen, tall and beautifully-figured."

"All right," I said, "It relates. So?"

"Katy was a problem, Mr. Chambers. Katy had to be handled very carefully. She was a stage-struck kid who wanted to be an actress. We encouraged it."

"Who's the we?"

"Vivian and myself, and a Dr. Kardon, a friend of mine, a psychiatrist. All during high school, Katy also attended dancing and dramatic school. It was a focal point for her energies. It—how shall I put it?—it held her in restraint."

"She needed—restraint?"

7

He shrugged. "At fifteen, Mr. Chambers, Katy was ready to run away from home."

"But why?"

"How the hell should I know why? Vivian found out about it and we, all of us, talked her out of it. That's when we began to encourage the acting thing. It held her—that, and my promise to her."

"Promise?"

"I wanted her to go to college, as Vivian had. She wanted no part of it—wanted no part of high school either, for that matter."

"What promise, Mr. Duff?"

"I promised that after she was graduated from high school, I'd let her come to New York, for a year. Sounds awful, doesn't it? That's why I gave you the background."

"Doesn't sound awful at all, sir." I was beginning to feel sorry for the guy. He was undressing and he was not the type to undress in front of a stranger and I was a stranger. "I'm with you, Mr. Duff," I said. "All the way."

"Thank you," he said, very humbly, for a banker.

"Not at all," I said, very humbly, for a private nothing.

"Five months ago, in June, she was graduated, and came along here to New York. She took an apartment, enrolled in the Kozko School of Dance, and enrolled with Stella Cullman for dramatics. I contacted Agatha Levine to do whatever she could for her."

"And what did Agatha do?"

"Got her an audition."

"Audition for what?"

"Flesh and Fury."

"Flesh and Fury!" I said.

Flesh and Fury was only the top musical on Broadway, sold out for the next year and a half, fifty bucks a copy for a single seat; that is, if you happened to be on intimate terms with the second wife of the first cousin of a canny speculator who had been lucky enough to have been on intimate terms with the first wife of the producer's father, and could prove all of that by voluminous affidavits developed in triplicate and signed in blood.

"The kid was good," Edward Duff said.

"How so?" I said.

"She got a job jumping around in the chorus, but much more important, the job was also as understudy to Suzy Lyons."

"Suzy Lyons?" I inquired in very mild tones.

"Suzy Lyons," he said in tones just as mild. "Which is why Agatha Levine recommended me to you in the first place."

"That Agatha Levine has got great big ears, hasn't she?"

"I wouldn't know," Edward Duff said.

"I happen to be out of my mind for Suzy Lyons," I said, "if that's any interest to you."

"My interest is Katy Duff."

"Shoot," I said. "You're the boss."

"I'll come to Suzy Lyons," he said.

"Over my dead body," I said.

"May I continue?" he said.

"By all means," I said.

"There were several provisions connected with my letting Katy come to New York," he said. "She was to write me at least one letter each week. She was to call me at home every Sunday. Plus I had arranged that I'd come here in December, transfer over to our New York office for a period of six months. Like that I'd be here, at least for the second half of her year, kind of in a supervisory capacity."

"Suppose," I said, "she was a star in that year. Or, much more likely, at least somewhere on her way to some kind of success?"

"That," he said, "was part of the deal. If she made, or was on her way toward making it—then she could continue in New York. If it went flat, then she'd come back to California, go to college and major in dramatics. At age twenty-one, she'd have the right to do whatever she pleased. So much," he said, "for background."

"Hold it a minute," I said.

"Yes?" he said.

"You said December, didn't you? That's when you were supposed to transfer here?"

"Yes."

"It's November now, or isn't it?"

"It is."

"Change of plans?"

"The change was precipitated for me."

"By Katy-gal?"

He nodded. "I was in Paris all of last month." He dug into his jacket pocket and placed four envelopes on my desk. "Her letters came through on schedule, one a week. But there were no phone calls."

"The letters came to your home?"

"Yes."

"Did she know you were going to Paris?"

"Yes, I'd told her during one of our Sunday talks."

"Well, did you expect her to call you all the way to Paris every Sunday?"

"No, of course not. Perhaps I thought she might have called through to Vivian—at least once—but on the whole, actually, I didn't really give it much thought. But this last Sunday—when she *knew* I'd be home—still no call."

9

"So, I take it, you called her."

"I did. Called all day Sunday. No answer."

"No show on Sunday," I said. "She could have gone out of town for the day, couldn't she?"

"Yes, she could have. But there was no answer on Monday either. I kept calling at intervals until four in the afternoon. No answer. That's when I called the production office."

"Production office?"

"Flesh and Fury."

"Sure. And what'd they tell you?"

"That she'd been granted a leave of absence."

I could feel the frown on my face. "When?" I said.

"That leave of absence was granted, Mr. Chambers, *one month ago!*"

TWO

H E STILL HAD the cigarette in his hand. He had not had time to light it. Now he had time. It was crumpled when he set it in his lips and his hand trembled when he lit it. He blew smoke at the match to extinguish it, dropped it into the ashtray, ran a hand through his hair and down his cheek. I let him smoke. I said nothing. I let him compose himself. I think he knew I was letting him compose himself and I think he appreciated it. His eyes moved over me, appraisingly. He had large dark eyes, but his eyes showed his age. They were filmy and a trifle bloodshot. More than a trifle, they were frightened. I let him smoke. He smoked. Then he said, "That was Monday."

"They told you when she was due back?"

"Yes. Wednesday. Tomorrow." He killed the cigarette. "I made my arrangements at once and flew out here. I'm here."

I pushed a finger at the four envelopes on my desk, separating them. "May I?" I said.

"Certainly," he said.

I took a letter out of each envelope. The handwriting was an imperious tall scrawl of backhand. I read through each letter quickly. I learned absolutely nothing. They were long and rambling and cute but they were about as informative as a recalcitrant defendant on trial for seduction. There was not one word about a leave of absence. I laid away the letters and sought information from the envelopes. All four were postmarked New York. "Took a leave of absence," I said, "and stayed right here in New York?"

"Curious, isn't it?" he said.

"Damn right," I said. "Why don't you wait until tomorrow and ask *her*, in person?"

"I don't want to ask her, in person."

"But why not?"

"I don't want to be in a position of a parent probing at his daughter. There are a delicate set of balances here, Mr. Chambers. Please, can't you understand that?"

"Yes, I think I can."

"I gave you the background."

"You sure did."

"I don't want this kid rearing up and breaking away. She's capable of that. I just don't want to upset the apple-cart, as it were. If she wants to tell me—great, fine. But if not—I still want to know. I . . . I'm desperately interested."

I sighed, a real deep one, from way back. I was glad I was not a parent. "Okay," I said. "You got into town today. What did you do?"

"Checked in at the office."

"Then?"

"Took over one of the company cars."

"Then?"

"Then I went to the Waldorf Towers and rented the suite that'll be my home for my stay in New York. Of course I kept calling Katy all the time. No answer."

"Suite at the Waldorf Towers," I said. "What suite?"

"2705."

"Then, after that?"

"I drove up to Agatha Levine's."

"Exactly what for?" I said.

"She knew about Katy, knew about me, knew about . . . the problem that is my Katy. It was Agatha, of course, who suggested you."

"Any special reason that she suggested me?"

"Suzy Lyons," he said.

"We're back to that, are we? Okay, then. Let's track it down. All the way. What's my love life got to do with your daughter?"

"Nothing." He moved about in his chair, uncomfortably.

"But that's twice now I got Suzy Lyons thrown at me."

"Katy adores Suzy Lyons."

"So?"

"She was the closest person to her here in New York."

"So?"

"Agatha felt that since you and Miss Lyons were quite friendly—"

"Big ears she's got, hasn't she?"

"She also said you were a brilliant man in your profession—"

"But that was incidental, wasn't it?"

"Not at all. It was just that it all fell into line. You were a friend of Miss Lyons, Miss Lyons was a friend of Katy's, the idea of a trustworthy private detective was an excellent one—"

"You're spending your thousand dollars so that I can pump Suzy for gossip about Katy." I opened the desk drawer and reached for the loot. "Respectfully," I said, "I decline." The hell with temptation.

"No! Please! Listen!" He lurched out of the chair, grabbed at the edge of the desk and leaned across. His knuckles were white. "Please," he said, "I'm not interested in gossip, I'm not interested in Suzy Lyons—I'm interested in a wonderful crazy kid who happens to be my daughter." He looked down at me almost fiercely, and I looked up at him almost contritely. "Please," he said, "I'm terribly worried. You can help me. Please help me. I tried to do what I thought was right for my daughter, I played along, I let her come here alone to New York, but I'm not sure, I'm not certain . . ." The filmy old eyes in the sunburnt young face tried to blink away tears.

"Mr. Duff," I said, "I'm a shmuck. Forgive me."

"Will you help? Please?"

"I'll do what the hell I can."

"Thank you."

"Forget it. You paid me, didn't you?"

"But please, it's imperative that she never know that I've checked on her, investigated. That kid would just blow up—"

"Of course, of course." I came out from behind my desk. "You've hired yourself what is euphemistically called a private richard, Mr. Duff. Suppose we begin at home base."

"Pardon?" He paced away.

"Where's her apartment?"

"334 East 78th. Apartment 12H." He kept pacing.

"She's not home, you say?"

"I'm certain she's not."

"Then suppose we open operations right there. We might get some hints, moseying around home base."

"I don't have a key."

"We can call on the superintendent. After all, you *are* her father, and you can prove it."

"No, that might leak back to her."

I smiled at him gloomily. "Mr. Duff, no matter how I try to avoid it, you're going to cost me money."

"Money's no object, Mr. Chambers. Any additional expense—"

"Frankly, I don't have the heart. Additional expenses, they'll come out of my fee. After all, she'll be back tomorrow, and you'll probably get all your answers without me." Dolorously I added, "It's going to cost me two hundred bucks."

12

"What's going to cost you?"

I got his coat and threw a roadblock into his pacing. I helped him on with his coat and gave him his hat. I grabbed my things and I asked him, "How's about a drink, Mr. Duff?"

"Love it," he said, "but I don't think I can drink two hundred dollars worth."

"You're going to," I said as I ushered him out.

At the elevator, I looked at my watch. It was six o'clock.

"Six o'clock," I said with brilliant extemporaneousness.

"And I'm double-parked, without lights."

"Those are expensive tickets in New York."

"I can afford it," he said.

It was sharp dark November cold outside, with a thick wind blowing snow from the north. We pulled our hats down low and walked against the snow until he yanked at my arm and pointed out the car. It was a shiny black Cadillac double-parked so far out that it created a hump in the traffic. But since Mr. Edward Duff could afford a ticket, there was no ticket. Wouldn't you know that? Those who can afford tickets never get tickets. It is a law of life.

"I'll drive," I said.

"Be my guest," he said.

In all the tank towns of America, throughout the bush leagues, in every cotton-picking hick-stick hamlet in the country, there is always a saloon with the egregiously original title of Oasis. There are more oases throughout the continental United States than have appeared in the mirages of parched travelers on every desert in all of time. In the great, big, bright, sophisticated metropolis of New York, I drove Mr. Edward Duff to Fifty-eighth and Second and we entered a watering place neon-emblazoned: OASIS. At the bar I inquired, "What'll your pleasure be, Mr. Duff?"

"For two hundred dollars?" he said.

"It's going to cost me," I said, "any way you interpret it."

"Bourbon," he said. "Water and lemon peel."

"Bourbon, water and peel," I said to the bartender, "for my friend. Brandy for me. Where's Zang?"

"Upstairs," the bartender said.

"Would you give him a buzz, please?"

"I'll be happy," the bartender said. "What's the name?"

"Peter Chambers."

"I'll be happy," the bartender said. "Drinks first or buzz first?"

"Drinks first, please."

"Who is Zang?" Edward Duff said.

Over bourbon and water and peel for him, and brandy for me, I told him. Zangwill Manchester was the only criminal I had ever met in whom were combined such dissimilar traits

13

as larceny, wisdom, business sense, and homespun philosophy. He was the only thief I had ever known who had set himself a goal for becoming honest, and had achieved his goal. Zang was a burglar who had plied his profession in the city of New York for eight long years and had not ever once even been arrested. The goal had been the accumulation of $200,000. When one considers that burglars steal objects rather than cash—clothes, jewels, furs—and that such objects, by dint of fences, are transposed to cash at a fraction of their intrinsic values, the fact that Zang had attained his goal within eight years stamped him as a man of singular diligence and constant effect. But Zang, unlike most criminous characters, kept the promise he had made to himself. He had retired from burglary when the nest egg had swelled to planned proportion. He had purchased a two-story building, created the Oasis downstairs, and set up domicile upstairs. The Oasis had thrived, and Zang was rich and respectable. He had never, however, disposed of his tool kit, an amazing box containing the most exquisite implements, from the most powerful of magnifying glasses to the most delicate of picklocks. Now and then, for those of his own particular inner circle, Zang did an odd job or two—not stealing, just obliging—but, as though not to lose his professional status, whatever was done was done for a price. It was even rumored that the long arm of the law crooked slightly, upon certain happenstance, in order to put Zang's unique talents to purpose.

"Buzz now," I said to the bartender.

The bartender went away.

"Remarkable," Duff said.

"Pardon?" I said.

"Zang," he said. "Will I meet him?"

"I hope," I said.

The bartender returned.

"Okay," the bartender said.

"Excuse me," I said to Edward Duff.

I went outside to the slender entrance adjacent to the doorway of the Oasis. I touched the one white anonymous button and the return click was almost instantaneous. I pushed in the bulky door, walked up a steep flight of stairs, knocked and Zang opened up for me.

"Come in, come in," he said heartily. "Long time no see and all the rest of that crap." He led me into a marvelously furnished Japanese living room. "Sit down," he said. "What do you want to drink?"

"Got Saki?" I said.

"Got everything," he said. "Piss, even. What's your pleasure, Peter?"

"Nothing, thanks," I said. "I'm working."

14

He was short, fat and bald with an apple-cheeked face and grinning eyes. He was impeccably dressed in a black suit, white shirt and black knit tie. "Working," he said. "Legal, I hope."

"Perfectly legal," I said.

"All right. What do you want, kid?"

"A little help."

"Like what, kid?"

"Like you should open a door for me. Maybe two doors."

"Legal?" he said.

"Perfectly legal," I said. "In fact my client is getting wet in your oasis downstairs."

"Who's your client?"

"Edward Duff. A banker from Beverly."

"Legit?" he said.

"A hundred percent."

"They pay pretty good, them bankers."

"Fair," I said.

"It's going to cost you, kid."

"Sure it will, Zangie dear. How much?"

"A couple of hundred. Plus I just open the doors. I don't even cross no threshold. I open up and good bye. What else you want?"

"Nothing else."

"I'll be able to stop in at your office for the cash payment?"

"Have I ever crossed you, Zangie lad?"

"Nope, or you wouldn't be here talking to me, kid."

"It'll be at my office. Any time starting tomorrow morning. My secretary will have the instructions."

"So okay, kid. So what are we waiting for?"

"You," I said.

He climbed into a grey cashmere coat, donned a pearl-grey homburg, left the room and returned with a little black bag.

Downstairs we collected Duff. I drove.

"Again?" Duff said. "Why you?"

"I know my way around this town. You're a stranger, remember?"

The banker, the richard, the thief-turned-tavern-owner—of the three, the thief-turned-tavern-owner looked most like a banker. Scratch that. What with his little black bag, he looked like a distinguished doctor, a specialist on his way to make an emergency house call: a brain specialist, at least.

"Friggin' snow," Zang said. "Who needs it?"

Brightly I said, "What do you expect? Plum trees? It's winter."

"Real sharp fella you hired yourself, Mr. Duff," Zang said.

East 78th Street was quietly residential. Except for the parked cars, the street was deserted save for an occasional hurrying figure. It was cold—the snow was not the leisurely big-flaked joyous kind—it was cold, bitter, icy, nostril-freezing nasty.

334 was tall, wide and old without canopy or doorman but with one obvious, if temporary, asset: a parking space directly in front sufficient to accommodate the length of a de luxe Caddy. I slid in and we got out. Zang put his gloves on.

The cramped lobby was steam-heated, with bells, brackets and buttons on a cracked marble wall to the right. Directly ahead was a glass door with a grill in front and curtains in back. I tried it. It was locked.

"Let's try in case the party is home," Zang said.

"You bet," I said.

The bracket of 12H held a neatly printed K. DUFF. I pressed the button, pressed again and again. The result was a broad smile from Zang and silence from the clicker.

"We could squeeze a few of the other buttons," Duff said. "Somebody'd tick back."

"That wouldn't be cricket," Zang said. "What's with cricket, anyway? Cricket's some kind of bug, ain't it?" He took an instrument from his bag and opened the door. "Got a hunch this little hunk of tempered steel is going to do the trick upstairs too."

Inside there was a wide frayed carpet, four tall distorted mirrors, and one automatic elevator. I looked about and looked to Duff. "Didn't you give her enough rent money?" I said.

"Let's say I wasn't spoiling her," Duff said. "As it happens, it's a sub-let. Three rooms at two hundred dollars a month. What was I going to do, buy her a house?"

"Yeah," Zang said. "The rents in New York—highway robbery."

The elevator took us to 12 without mishap. Zang thrust a look at the lock of H and smiled. "My hunch was correct," he said. "I'm stealing your money, kid. Make it up to you some other time." He maneuvered steel against brass for a short moment, and opened the door for us. "Me," he said, "I don't even cross the threshold. Enjoy yourself, gentlemen."

He bowed, waved and departed.

Duff preceded me. I closed the door. We were in darkness. There was no sound except the sound of our breathing. My hand crawled along the wall seeking the light switch. I found it and clicked it. Overhead light showed us a small, well-furnished, square vestibule, with a thick red rug. To the left was an archway leading into a step-down parlor. From

16

our angle we could only see a tangent of it. It had the same red rug as the vestibule.

This trip, I preceded Duff. I flicked the parlor switch and we got light from an elaborate high-hung chandelier. It was a tremendous room. Whoever had sub-let to Katy had had a choice apartment in an old building when they had built their rooms for people and not for murphy-bed midgets. It was vast and it was exquisitely furnished but our eyes went instantly to a massive brocaded couch which faced us from the far end of the room.

A man was seated in one corner of the couch. He was slender and smiling and exceedingly handsome. He was dark and pale with sparkling white teeth. He wore a navy-blue suit, a tab-collared white shirt and a dark conservative tie. His right elbow rested on the right arm of the couch and the fingers of his right hand were clasped about the butt of a thick black automatic.

The thick black automatic was pointed at us.

THREE

In the utter silence of the room, Duff's half-gasp behind me sounded like the blast of a train-whistle in a tunnel, but I gave it no heed. My entire heed was being devoted to the smiling young man with the gun. I recognized him and I hoped, fervently, that he recognized me. His name was Allan Sylvester, man about New York town, a virile specimen of male pulchritude, but as virulent a specimen as a two-headed cobra with a large hate for each head. Allan Sylvester once appeared on television before a Senate Investigating Committee—investigating rackets—and he was the young man who proclaimed to the world that he had garnered a large share of the world's goods by virtue of having devised a foolproof system to beat the horses. Whether or not this was true, there was no question that Allan Sylvester kept reaping of the world's goods without performing one single act of legitimate labor. Allan Sylvester was a handsome parasite, a dangerous bloodsucker, a leech upon women and a drain upon men, and Allan Sylvester with a gun in his hand was as attractive to me as an oncoming kangaroo carrying radioactive fallout in its pouch.

"Hi, Allan," I heard myself murmuring, weakly.

The young man continued to smile but he made no acknowledgment.

"You know him?" Duff whispered behind me.

"I do," I said. "Hi, Allan."

The young man offered no reply.

17

A trickle of presentiment ran down my spine like a rivulet of sweat. I admit that I lacked the courage to proceed pell mell in the direction of the pointing gun but a dreadful suspicion arose within me that if I did proceed I could come to no harm. I did not proceed because when there exists a risk, however slight, that I might accumulate small holes in my body, I am rather cautious. I stood rooted but I peered more closely at the handsome young man of Manhattan. True, the smile sparkled, but that was only because the teeth were sheer white and reflected light from the chandelier. There was no mirth in the expression of the face and from where I stood the eyes showed no recognition, they showed only glassiness. Also, although paleness is consistent with the indoor type of city man in winter, Allan's paleness, on closer study, was an unnatural paleness, a peculiar pallor kind of paleness. But as I stretched my hand to keep Duff from coming forward, I watched the eyes. And after a few moments, I was real brave. I moved forward. Tentatively, I admit—but I moved.

The eyes had not blinked.

When I got to him, I touched him.

"This guy's dead," I said.

"No," Duff said behind me.

"Dead," I said. "But not dead long. The son of a bitch is still warm." I reached down and touched the hand holding the gun. It was rigid.

"Suicide?" Duff said behind me.

"How the hell would I know?" I said.

I stood back and looked him over. He was securely snuggled in a corner of the couch and that held him up. Suicide? Possibly. You kill yourself and you fall into your position of death and your position of death may be a menacing one since your right hand is clenched about a gun and your elbow is supported by the arm of the couch. But where was the bullet hole? I bent and I peered and I found it. The fashionable navy-blue suit, single-breasted and with charming lapels, had a small hole on the left side parallel to the middle button. I opened the button and laid back the jacket. The white shirt showed a crust of blood, still red. I drew a deep breath and straightened up. I took off my hat to scratch my head. I do not believe I should have. I never got to scratch my head and that is an ache that still remains with me. Instead, a thump happened. It happened, solidly and accurately, over my left ear. I keeled over, perhaps gracefully.

I remember hitting the rug.

And then memory vanished.

FOUR

DID YOU EVER smell a rug?

It smells of dust.

Did you ever smell dust?

It has a smell of its own. It is indescribable, but it has a smell of its own. Try it sometime. Lie down on a rug, prone, with your nose imbedded, and take a deep breath. You will smell dust and you will know what I mean about the special smell of dust in a rug.

I smelled it. I smelled it for some time before I realized I was smelling it. I lay prone with my nose imbedded breathing the odor of dust and rug, already conscious, but unaware of the fact. Listlessly I lay there like an elderly husband after a frantic honeymoon, and then I sneezed, and that brought me up to my knees, ludicrously quadruped, moving my head and looking upward like a hound with no moon to bay at. I sneezed again and I got to my feet ruminatively rubbing a hand at the welt over my left ear. Recollection rushed back like water through a burst dam, and I was angry.

I banked my anger.

I looked about.

The room was neat and orderly except for the candlestick on the floor beside me. There was no sign of Allan Sylvester and no sign of Edward Duff. I looked again at the candlestick on the floor and appreciated from whence had been produced the welt behind my ear. I lifted the candlestick and replaced it equidistant from its sister candlestick on the mantel over a spurious city-type fireplace. Then I reviewed the apartment. That gave me nothing more than a fairly good wardrobe for a fairly tall dame. From the color of the clothes she figured to be a brunette. Big deal. Real astute detective. I quit the apartment and went out into the snow.

I trudged, thinking, conscious of a small pain over my left ear. My thinking added up to nothing more than the disappearance of a dead con merchant and a live banker. Again I experienced anger. Again I suppressed it. I entered a cigar store, purchased two packs of suspiciously cancerous filter-type cigarettes (of which I smoked four packs a day and the hell with the cancer) and used the change to make a phone call. I called the Waldorf and asked for Edward Duff and got a good deal of clicking and then a monotonous ringing in my ear, but I got no answer. I hung up and called my own apartment. It rang until the Service answered, which, if you have a Service, takes a hell of a long time. But I had patience.

"Peter Chambers' apartment," said the utterly disinterested voice.

"Any calls for me?" I said.

"Who're you?" said the tired voice.

"Guess," I said.

"Peter Chambers' apartment," sang the tired voice.

"Any calls for me?" I said.

"Who is this, please?" said the tired voice.

"Mr. Chambers," I said.

"Oh, hi,'" said the voice, swelling one notch from abysmal boredom.

"Any messages?" I said.

"Just one moment, please."

I waited three full minutes while the clicks in my ear were like a form of Chinese torture. For this, I thought, I pay thirty-five bucks a month—go do something! Finally the fatigued voice returned. "Hello! Peter Chambers' apartment."

"Remember me, honey?" I said. "Same fella. Mr. Chambers."

"Oh, hi, Mr. Chambers."

"Any messages for me?"

"A Mr. Duff called. For you to call him back."

"Thanks," I said. "A large lump."

"Oh, don't mention it, Mr. Chambers."

I hung up. I called Duff. There was no answer.

I took a cab back to my apartment. I called Duff. There was no answer. I stripped down naked and took a long warm shower. I washed my body with lots of soap and washed my hair with the latest advertised shampoo. I dried with the latest advertised towels and spread the latest advertised body lotion over my latest advertised body. Then, naked, I went back to the living room. There was enough hissing steam to keep me warm had I shed my skin. I used a hand mirror against the full-length mirror in the living room to examine the pain behind my ear. It was a lump, somewhat bruised, but without abrasion. But being, as all Americans, antiseptically conditioned, I went back to the bathroom and dabbed witch hazel on my lump. Then I went back to the living room, sprawled out on the couch, picked up the phone and called Edward Duff.

No answer.

I put back the receiver and I dozed.

No sooner was I embroiled in a lusciously pornographic

20

dream, when the phone rang. Wouldn't you know? I reached out a lazy hand for the receiver and said in my most lusciously pornographic voice, "Yeah? Who is it?"

"Hi, lover," said Suzy Lyons.

The pornographic dream ceased. The dream, this is. "Only beloved," I said, "I've been waiting all day. Where've you been?"

"Waiting for you to call," she said, "only beloved."

"I called," I lied.

"That's a big lie," she said.

"Like that a lady talks?" I said.

"I love you," she said.

"I love you," I said. "Supper after the show at Royal?"

"That's why I'm calling," she said. "We skip the supper tonight."

"Only beloved," I said, "have you got yourself another only beloved?"

"You think I'm out of my mind?" she said.

"Where are you?" I said.

"At the theatre. It's five minutes before curtain."

"So it is," I said without looking at my watch which I was not wearing. "So what's with cancelling supper, only beloved?"

"I've got to go out to the airport," she said, "after the show."

"So what's wrong with supper after the show after the airport? I'm easy to get along with."

"You've got a party to go to," she said.

"Without you," I said, "I go nowhere." I am nothing if not a temporarily faithful swain. And with Suzy Lyons you didn't have to work at it to be temporarily faithful.

"I love you," she said.

"I love you," I said. "So what party do I have to go to? And I'm not going without you."

"Who said you're going without me?"

"Then I'm going," I said. "Where do I pick you up?"

"You don't," she said.

"Then the hell with the party, only beloved. If you insist on talking in riddles with your curtain five minutes away—"

"Shut up, please! Listen!"

"I'm shut," I said. "I'm listening. Fervently."

Her melodious voice took on didactic overtones. "There is a party," she said, "at Freddie Flanders' house. I'm invited. You're invited. It's for after the show. I must go out to the airport to pick someone up. I shall go out to the airport to pick that someone up. You, in the meantime, will go to the party. You should be there, in propriety, by midnight. And there, at the party, sooner or later, I shall join

21

you. Now, if you please, would you like me to translate this for you into early Hebrew, or perhaps you'd like it Turkish style?"

"With you, sweetheart, I like it all styles."

"Got to go now, my adventurous lover," she said. "Oh! It's black tie. So exhume that moth-eaten tuxedo."

"Moth-eaten my ass," I said. "You know very well I've got a brand new creation fashioned by none other than Mack Berger, the sexiest tailor in all New York town—"

"Wear it," she said and daintily disconnected.

I hung up, slowly. I sighed, slowly. Thoughts about Suzy Lyons wafted deliciously within me and I slowly stretched and wriggled my toes and uttered foolish little animal grunts and then, of course, the phone rang. I lifted the thing to my ear and despondently I intoned, "All right, all right, enough already, I'll be waiting at that goddamned party—"

"Mr. Chambers!" Edward Duff's voice was slightly incredulous.

"You're a sly old son of a bitch, aren't you?" I said.

"I called you." he said. "You weren't home."

"I was sleeping," I said, "with my nose in your daughter's rug."

"I called you," he repeated. "You weren't home."

I flung my feet off the couch. "I called you back, old bastard," I said. "You weren't home either. Where are you?"

"Home," he said.

"Home is the hotel?" I said.

"I'm at the hotel," he said.

"I called you," I said. "You weren't there."

"I just got back. I want to talk to you."

"Well, goddamn it, man, you *are* talking to me, aren't you?"

"I want to talk to you personally."

"Personally? Like you can hit me a shot in the head the minute my back is turned? Is that what you mean?"

"Will you come here, please, Mr. Chambers?"

"Pal, I'm coming, you can depend on that. If you'll only stay put."

"I'll be here the rest of the night, Mr. Chambers."

"You'd better be, Mr. Banker, else you'll have more cops around you than you've got capital gains schemes for your clients." And with that I hung up on him. I hung up hard. You cannot hit an old man even though he has raised a bump at the left rear of your hairline. So you do it symbolically. You belt him electronically. You hit him with the telephone. I admit it is small satisfaction, but don't we all reconcile ourselves with small satisfactions as we compromise our way to eternity?

I got up off my couch with all the energy of a reluctant patient ending his fifty-minute hour with his favorite psychiatrist. I showered again and maybe that was symbolic too. Then I shaved. I made my face smooth of bristles and I dabbed at it with masculine-scented feminine-attractive perfumes. Between you and me, they stank. I squeezed at a couple of blackheads, batted my eyes at my eyes in the mirror, scratched at various strategic spots on my body, brushed my hair to bring out the last reluctant wave, urinated moodily, and dressed. I surveyed myself in the full-length mirror and I grudgingly acquiesced with Mack Berger's sartorial philosophy that dress-shirt and well-cut dinner jacket do more for the crumbling male than slacks and sports shirt with its tail hanging out. Then I spat at the mirror, doused the lights, locked up, and merrily hied off to the Towers of the Waldorf.

Not too merrily, I submit.

I was, after all, stone sober.

FIVE

EDWARD DUFF OPENED the door for me and smiled in greeting. The smile was as limp as the back row of burlesque. He was wearing a maroon smoking jacket with satin lapels and a satin belt. He held himself upright as he escorted me to the living room but you had the feeling that if he loosened the hold on his spine he would crumple. He took my hat and coat and his eyes swept over me. "Formal?" he said and he squinted as though trying to understand it.

"You go formal," I said, "when you call on a banker. It's an ancient New York custom. Especially when you call on a banker who has recently kidnapped a corpse."

"We're going to talk about that."

"You bet your sweet ass," I said.

"Would you like a drink?" he said.

"I would love a drink," I said. "Lots of Scotch and a little water."

"Please sit down," he said.

I sat. He splashed the drink for me from an ornate cabinet. He took nothing for himself. He handed me the glass and he sat down in an easy chair. He put his hands over his face and began to cry. I gulped the drink like it was medicine. He had used so much Scotch and so little water it tasted like medicine. I gulped my medicine and watched him cry and inside myself I cried too. This was no footling adolescent. This was no pawky actor playing a role to wrest sympathy. This was a grown, contained man, engulfed by an emotion, and fighting against engulfment. In his effort to control himself, he made gasping, retching, terrible sounds, his entire body trembling, his knees moving up as though striving for the position of the embryo, his shuddering shoulders rising up as though to encircle and hide the already hidden face behind the masking hands.

"Cut it out," I said. "Please. Cut it out."

It was enough to drive you to drink. It drove me to drink. I drank. I knocked off that highball like it was soothing cream and I was burning with an ulcer. "Forget it," I said. "Please. Stop it." Whether or not he knew it, Edward Duff and I were all even, throbbing bump over my left ear or no.

I went to the cabinet for more medicine.

He ceased producing his awful sounds.

He rose out of his chair and turned his back to me. He used a handkerchief to wipe his face and blow his nose.

"I'm sorry," he said without facing me.

"Forget it," I said. "Where's Sylvester?"

"Who is Sylvester?"

"Who is Sylvia?" I said.

"What?" he said.

"Sylvester is a hoodlum," I said. "What did you do with him?"

"Pardon me," he said.

He left the room. While I stole another drink, a short one, I heard him in the bathroom. He was washing his face. He was also probably wiping his face and combing his hair and killing enough time to come back to some type of personal orderliness. I did not interfere. I snatched more of his Scotch. I was limbering up. After all, I was going to a party tonight. If it was at Freddie Flanders' house it would be a drink-type party. Compared to Freddie Flanders, as concerned the imbibation of hard liquor, I was a rank amateur. But Freddie Flanders had a right to his idiosyncrasies. Freddie Flanders was a genius. Me? I'm no genius.

Edward Duff re-appeared in his living room trying hard to place a smile on his face. "Please forgive me," he said.

"The hell with it," I said. "Where's our suicide?"

"He wasn't a suicide," he said.

"Mr. Duff," I said, "you're a banker, not a criminologist. You wouldn't know."

"I know," he said.

"Okay," I said, "you had yourself a nice good cry, and if you'd like, I'll have myself a nice good cry, but after that, you and me, let's get down to cases."

"Like this?" he said and he stuffed a hand into the pocket of his smoking jacket and brought it out with an oblong of paper which he handed to me. I accepted it and studied it. It was a check drawn to the order of Peter Chambers,

24

signed by Edward Duff, to the ringing tune of five thousand dollars.

"You've been reading the wrong books, Mr. Duff," I said. "There are private detectives and private detectives. There are moral ones and immoral ones. Essentially, and it may be a great big secret, I'm a moral one. I don't accept the bribes of transgressors. Even when the bribe is five thousand bananas. Thanks a great group, but I decline."

"It's not a bribe," he said.

"What else *can* it be?" I said.

"Look," he said. "This is no longer a simple investigation into a young girl's whereabouts. This is murder. I don't know whether or not she is mixed up in it, but either way, I need help. I'm paying you in advance for that help."

"But I'm not mixing up with whatever you pulled with Allan Sylvester."

"I'm not asking you to mix into that."

"I'm mixed already," I said grimly.

"How?"

"I'm an accessory, unless we go to the cops with it right now."

"We're not going."

"Then that five thousand bucks is a bribe, isn't it, no matter how we try to couch it in more respectable terms."

"No, it's not."

"Then what the hell is it?"

"I told you."

"And I told *you*."

"Chambers, please listen to me." He folded his hands behind his back and kicked at the carpet as he strode about. "Once more I'm thinking about a kid seventeen and a half years of age. If she did this thing, or she's associated with it—by all means, the law shall take its course. I promise you that. But, if, by some chance, she's not actually involved, then I want to save her from the kind of scandal that can knock the props right out from under her, that can mess up her life practically at its beginning. I'm trying to protect her from that."

"But how?"

"First I want to talk to her."

"Sure. Of course," I said.

"If she's involved—for whatever reason—I'll hear her story, get her a lawyer, and bring her in, I swear to you. And of course I'll confess to my part in this."

"What about me?"

"I'll leave you out of it."

"How'll you say you got into that apartment?"

"I'll say I had a key."

"And when they'll ask you to produce it?"

"I shall be able to produce it."

"*What?*" I said. "All this time you *had* a key?"

"Not all this time. But I have one now."

"When'd you get it?"

"I'll come to that."

"Man, it takes you a hell of a long time to spin out a yarn." I lit a cigarette. "What happens on that million to one shot—that she's not involved?"

"Then I want time."

"Time? Time for what?"

"Time to work it out. Time to prevent a scandal. Time for you, perhaps, to solve this crime, and to give us something, somehow, that we can use as barter material with the police."

"Barter for what?"

"For keeping my daughter's name out of this, out of the public prints. Perhaps, even, the police will solve it—"

"Fat chance. With you obstructing justice."

"Believe me, Mr. Chambers, I'm not trying to obstruct justice." He came to me and put his hands on my arms. I could feel them tremble. "I'm trying to do what I can for my kid. If she's got anything to do with this, I'll bring her to the law myself. But on that million to one shot that she hasn't, then I beg of you, please help me."

I shook him off and now I strode his carpet. Down deep, I admired the guy. He was a fighter, and I admired a fighter. He was the parent of a problem daughter and the weight of that had suddenly hit him two-fold: first her disappearance, and then the dead Sylvester propped up on her couch. He was a worried man who loved his child and he had tried to do what he had thought was right for her, but he was far from certain that what he had done *was* right for her. Maybe she was just a lousy little tramp—there are a lot of them, young ones, and from good families—or maybe she was a good kid suffering from lack of mother—

"Wild," he said as though reading my thoughts. "Crazy wild, but I'd take an oath, not really bad, not rotten, evil, vicious . . ."

I folded his check and stuffed it into my pocket. "You talked me into it," I said. "I hope it doesn't wind up trouble. For me."

"I promise you," he said.

"Skip it," I said. "I'm your boy. I ought to have my head examined."

"Thank you, Mr. Chambers."

His hands clenched and unclenched. He looked as though he were going to cry again. Hurriedly I said, "All right. What happened up there on 78th Street?"

26

"I . . . I acted on instinct."

"Some instinct," I said as I gloomily patted the mastoid region over my left ear.

"If we reported it, we'd have the police, and if we had the police, Katy would be irrevocably involved in it, innocent or no. So, first, I wanted him out of there. That would give me time, one way or the other. I knew you wouldn't agree."

"You knew so damned right, brother."

"So I made use of that candlestick on the mantel. I tried not to hit you too hard. There was no malice in it, you understand."

"Thanks a lump," I said. "Okay, you didn't hit me too hard. Then what?"

"His hat and coat were hanging in the closet. I dressed him and got him out of there. It was not too difficult. The snow was like a shield, and the car was right out front. It was as though I were helping a drunken friend."

"Then you drove off."

"Yes."

"Where?"

"I don't know. Uptown. I crossed the bridge at 138th Street. I was in the Bronx, I think."

"You were in the Bronx. Then?"

"I came to an area where there was construction work going on in the daytime. It was quiet, deserted. I parked. I emptied his pockets and then I carried him out and laid him away."

"Great," I said. "Maybe you should have been an undertaker rather than a banker. Okay, then what?"

"I drove back into town. Went to a drugstore, checked your home phone in the directory, called you. You weren't in yet, but your Service answered. I left a message for you to call me."

"I called you. You weren't in either."

"I was in for a while."

"You came back here?" I said.

"But then I went out again," he said.

"Why?" I said.

"Come here, Mr. Chambers," he said.

He led me into a bedroom. He pointed to a group of items on top of a chest of drawers. With a poking forefinger I ungrouped the group. In order of pokes they were: one handkerchief, one pack of cigarettes, three packs of matches, one lighter, one automatic pistol, one leather packet of keys, one single key, one wrist watch, ninety-two cents in change, one small comb, one thin wallet containing a driver's license and two hundred and twelve dollars.

"That's how I knew he wasn't a suicide," Duff said.

27

"Like how did you know?"

He took the clip out of the automatic and showed me. It was full. "He was murdered," he said.

"Yeah," I said. "And with a gun in his hand. So it was unexpected."

"You thinking of Katy?" Duff said.

"I'm merely stating a fact," I said. "So why didn't you stay here?"

"This," he said and he lifted the single key.

"Very enigmatic," I said. "Please continue."

"I wondered," he said, "about that single key. There was that leather container of keys, and this single key. I wondered about that single key."

"Like maybe Katy had given the boy a key. No question he was a handsome bastard."

"Yes," he said unhappily.

"So?" I said.

"I went back there with this single key. It opened the downstairs door and it opened the door to her apartment. That's how he got in there. He had a key."

"I don't want to be cruel," I said, "but do you think maybe Katy had a lover?"

"I don't know. It's possible. I don't know."

"Skip," I said. "Then you came back here?"

"No."

"A compulsion to fly around the town, huh?"

"This time I flew because of you."

"Me?" I said and peered at him.

"I realized, sooner or later, I was going to have to explain to the police. I didn't want to involve you. If I had a key, I wouldn't have to involve you. I'd say—and I'd have Katy say—that she'd given me a duplicate. So I drove around again until I found an open hardware store and I had a duplicate made." He replaced everything on the chest of drawers, slid a hand into his pants pocket and produced a key. "This," he said.

"I appreciate it," I said. "Anything else?"

"That's all."

"It's plenty." My chuckle was like a belch.

Silence. Silence all the way back to the living room.

"Would you like to have supper with me?" I said.

"No, thank you."

"You going to stay put?"

"Yes. Right here."

"Good enough." I looked at my watch. "In case of any emergency, I'll be at Royal House. That's a restaurant. I'll be there until about midnight. After that, I'll be at a party at Freddie Flanders' town house. You can reach me at

28

either place. I'm on call for you. I'm your boy. Six thousand dollars' worth minus two hundred to Zang." I went for my hat and coat.

"Freddie Flanders?" Duff said.

"Freddie Flanders," I said. "Man genius. Writer, director, producer of a shabby little enterprise entitled *Flesh and Fury.*"

"Party at Freddie Flanders," he said, eyebrows up.

I had finally made a hit with my client.

SIX

I WENT TO Royal House at Fifty-seventh and Park. I went to Royal House because I was wearing a tuxedo but that was not the only reason. I mean the food in Bertha's Beanery is just piquant but if you show up at Bertha's at eleven-thirty in a tuxedo you simply do not fit. You can get a coffee cup hurled at you across the counter just for the joke of it; certainly, the whistles from the assorted fruits sitting around lapping coffee and quoting Kafka and Camus can disconcert you. Of course there are other fancy saloons—pardon me, supper clubs—where you can have late supper while strapped into a dinner jacket, but Royal House, for me, had become routine because of Suzy Lyons. Suzy Lyons was a principal in *Flesh and Fury* and the principals of *Flesh and Fury,* and also the bosses, ate, after the show, exclusively at Royal House.

Royal House boasted a chef named Dominique who had been lured from a one-arm joint called Tour D'Argent out of a hamlet called Paris set in a country called France. Dominique, I have heard tell, brought in the gourmets from far and wide. Also the gourmands. Also the epicures, whatever they may be. That Dominique had more pulling power than a lush-lipped movie actress breast-acting across a wide screen without a girdle in real-life color. But Royal House had a shot and a follow-up. Aside from Dominique, Royal House also boasted its owner, Tony Royal, and Tony Royal was a character. A restaurant owned by a character is like a book written by an under-age nymphomaniac. It assures its popularity. Once upon a time, when Royal House was Tootsie's, Tony Royal had been its doorman. When Royal House was Tootsie's it served nothing more exotic than steaks and chops but since it was owned by a character it was also popular. The character was an elderly gent named Toots Applebaum who had been a heavyweight contender fighting under the name of Hurricane Bumble. Toots had saved his money and after his last knockout had moved on to the cemetery of all ex-prizefighters, a restaurant. Toots had certain of the ephemeral requisites that go to make up the successful restaurateur. He clapped his male guests on the back with sufficient heartiness to shake up their lungs, and his ingenuous profanity to his lady guests established him as an "absolute darling." So Tootsie's flourished and the visiting firemen waited in line to get in. They'd have done better having the old lady fry them a veal cutlet over the electric stove in the hotel bedroom.

Anyway, Toots was fond of Tony and promoted him from doorman to waiter, and from waiter to maître d', and from maître d' to manager, and from manager to intimate friend. Toots was unmarried and without relatives and when senility set in, in the form of arthritis, Tony nursed him while honestly caring for the restaurant. Toots died, and his will left forty thousand dollars in cash to Tony, plus Tootsie's. Tony closed the joint, refurbished it, imported Dominique, and opened up as Royal House. Tony was the best of business men and his restaurant was truly a gem.

I checked my hat and coat and checked into Royal House. Tony Royal, in exquisite tuxedo, greeted me.

"Hi," he said. "Ain't you going to the party?"

"I am," I said, "but first I feed."

"Yeah, man," he said. "Ain't many of the regulars here tonight."

"Don't figure," I said as I followed him to a table.

Of the regulars, Joel Barker was seated at a corner table with Janet Lewis, and Linda Moreno was regally alone at the table of honor. Barker was co-producer with Flanders of *Flesh and Fury*, Janet was in the chorus but was understudy to the star, and Linda Moreno was the star. Linda waved to me and I waved back but I did not join her. I loved Suzy and Linda was a man-eater, so who needs the trouble that even the most idle of gossip can bring.

Tony brought me to a table and sat down with me. Tony was a handsome black-haired blue-jawed man with sturdy shoulders and thick hands. Tony had a soft voice and a hard temper and he wore an enormous star sapphire ring on the middle finger of his right hand. A star sapphire, properly propelled, can be as lethal as brass knuckles.

A waiter came with a menu and Tony said, "What'll it be, pal?"

"Ham and eggs," I said.

"Ham and eggs! With the great Dominique in the kitchen!"

"Country style," I said.

"Man, you're a card, ain't you?"

"I think you're the card, Tony."

"Ham and eggs, country style," Tony said to the waiter. "Make that two orders. Man, I ain't had ham and eggs country style since I own this goddam bistro. We'll come to your crack about me being a card," he said to me, "after we have a couple of drinks." To the waiter he said, "Double Scotch for my friend, double Scotch for me, before the ham and eggs. And tell them hash brown on the country style."

When the double Scotches appeared, gleaming amidst the gleaming silverware, Tony stirred with swizzle stick and inquired, "What's with me a card, pal?"

"Linda Moreno," I said and sipped.

"How come you don't keep your nose clean, pal?"

"I'm keeping it clean. You asked, I'm happy to tell you. You want me not to tell you, I won't. But whether you realize it or not, people wonder."

"About what?"

"About you."

"Meaning about me and Linda?"

"Meaning exactly that."

We both looked toward her table. Nick Wallace, in dinner clothes, had just come in and seated himself beside her. Nick Wallace was the press agent for *Flesh and Fury*. But we were not looking at Nick. We were looking at Linda Moreno. She was black and white: white skin, enormous black eyes, and shining black hair parted in the middle and drawn to a bun in back. Linda had been born in England, achieved a measure of success as a dancer and singer, and had, at twenty, married an Argentinean. She had removed to Buenos Aires, had there divorced her husband, and had there reached full stature as a star. At twenty-nine, she had come to New York, and here she had been discovered by Freddie Flanders. She had been discovered by Freddie, in point of fact, in this very room—Royal House. She had been introduced to Freddie by Tony Royal. At that time it had been known about New York that Linda Moreno and Tony Royal were lovers. It was now known about New York that Linda Moreno was Freddie Flanders' mistress.

"You mean people talk about me, Linda, Freddie?" Tony said.

"I mean it was a kind of smooth transition."

"Whatever the hell that means."

"From Tony to Freddie without a murmur from Tony."

"Why should I murmur?"

"Do you hate him, Tony?"

"Why should I be an exception? Everybody hates him, he's that kind of guy. Take his partner Barker over there, or Janet Lewis, or even Linda herself—they all hate him. Me?" Strong teeth showed in a stony grin. "I dunno. But I think you're full of crap about people talking."

Nick Wallace sat down beside us. "You guys look like

31

you're arguing," he said. "Anything interesting?" He was small and slender with brown eyes, brown hair and a brown face merging to a sort of nondescript anonymity, but he had nervous jaw muscles.

"Ask Nick," I said, "as long as we're talking about it."

"Ask me what?" Nick said.

Tony rubbed at his star sapphire. "Do people talk?"

"About what?"

"Me. Linda. Freddie Flanders."

Nick smiled. Even his teeth were brown. He drew out a cigarette and lit it. "Only that you're a funny guy, Tony," he said. "Fella steals your girl and you seem to be happy about it."

"Why, you son of a bitch," Tony said. Tony was a business man right down deep into his soul. He never argued with people whom he respected—perhaps he respected me. But he did not respect Nick Wallace. To him Nick was nothing, a flack, lint that Freddie Flanders brushed off his cuff. "*You're* talking, you son of a bitch. You, a lousy beard. You're criticizing me?"

A "beard," in the parlance, is a cover-up for a married man with a sweetheart. The "beard" serves as the lady's escort and is always the third man present at social functions attended by the married man and the lady. For the world, the "beard"—unmarried and respectable—is the properly functioning boy friend for the lady.

"I'm not criticizing," Nick said mildly.

"You, her phony boy friend!"

"Hell," Nick said, "I work for the guy. I get two hundred clams a week and I don't break my back to earn it. So, I squire her around, and Freddie picks up the tab. What've I got to lose?"

"It's like a pimp," Tony said.

"Oh my, shame, shame, shame," Nick said, winking at me.

Tony looked from one to the other of us. His smile was somewhat anxious. "Look. You guys kidding me?"

"A little bit," I said. "A little bit not."

"I think I can explain it," Tony said.

"Why don't you?" I said. "Get it off your chest."

"Look, that Linda Moreno, a terrific hunk, I admit it. I ought to know. I been around. Plenty."

"So?" Nick said.

"But that one can eat you up alive. She can take on the three of us and come back for an encore. Don't tell me, Nickie-boy, she ain't made a play for you already?"

"Even if she did, I wouldn't know it. Like that, kid, I'm unconscious. All the way. I know on what side my bread is buttered."

32

"Me too," Tony said, "if you figure it."

"I don't figure it," I said. "You still overboard for that chick? The truth, Tony."

"Sure I am."

"And still you have no hard feelings?" Nick said.

"Lemme explain it, huh?"

"Sure, Tony."

"First, who's Tony? Who am I? A doorman that Toots Applebaum happened to like. So I fall into a restaurant, but I'm what you call a host, a natural-type host. Okay, so I begin to spread out a little bit, me and my Dominique, and the interior decorator who did this joint, and I begin to become a little bit of a big-shot in the business."

"Don't be modest," I said. "A big big-shot. Royal House is one of the top."

"So okay. So how do I get there? Lemme tell you how. By knowing how to handle the best, that's how. By getting real friendly with the best, that's how. And Freddie Flanders, that's one of the best. You guys know as well as I do, that baby's good for fifteen, twenty gees a year here, him and his parties, and the fancy drinking, champagne for everybody. With guys like that you don't fight, not if you're a good business man."

"And you're nothing if not a good business man," Nick said dryly. "So?"

"So I'm stuck on this Linda. So, months ago, Freddie meets her, and *he's* stuck on her. So how do we stack, me and Freddie? Me? I'm Tony Royal, ex-doorman, period. Freddie? He's a millionaire, many times over, even got mentioned in Fortune magazine. He's a famous name all over the world. For twenty-five years this guy's been knocking out hit shows one after another. Got class, got talent, got brains. And that crazy memory of his—why he could go on the stage as a magician with that crazy memory of his."

"I think," Nick said, "of all things, he's proudest of that crazy memory of his." He blew his cigarette smoke at me. "You know, he can quote, word for word, from a play of his that's twenty years old. And when he's really loaded— and trying to prove that he isn't—you should hear the fantastic quotes he comes up with. Fabulous, that Freddie Flanders."

"Fabulous Freddie Flanders," Tony said. "So how does Tony Royal with the fancy name stack up against fabulous Freddie Flanders? Tony can't win, so Tony's smart enough to back out. Plus Freddie was casting for *Flesh and Fury* and Linda Moreno was a natural for the lead. So, if I fight him—I lose a customer, I lose a friend, and sooner or later I lose that dame anyway because who the hell can hold a mad one like that?"

"Not even Freddie?" Nick said.

"Are you kidding, Nickie boy? Freddie's an old man, and a tired old man, which is why he's always looking for young chicks, the youngest."

"Linda's not so young," Nick said with a mild bite.

"Linda was a gorgeous hunk that he had to capture. But he don't stay true to her like he don't stay true to his wife. He's always looking for the young chicks." To me he said, "So watch out for Suzy."

"I've watched. I don't stop watching," I said. "With Suzy he doesn't rate. Suzy's too smart."

"Too smart," Tony said, returning rib for rib, "because she picked you?"

"Too smart," I said, "because she didn't pick him."

"A tired old man," Tony said. "He hates it. That's what's always eating into him. Yeah, *he* can play around, but not his chicks, oh no. He's jealous, old-man jealous, which is why he whiplashes everybody. He's an angry man, angry at getting old."

"You're a pretty good philosopher," I said admiringly. "Or is it a pretty good psychologist?"

"Pretty good nothing," he said. "I'm an ex-doorman, period. But I can figure people, it's kind of part of my business. And when it comes to Linda, brother, he whiplashes her most of all, because he knows in his heart—that one he cannot really hold, at all."

"According to you," Nick said, "who can?"

Tony disregarded that. "And he's afraid of her too," he said. "Crapping in his pants. That bambino's got a temper, she can kill a guy. The way he treats her, he's liable to wind up that romance with a bottle over his head, with his skull split."

"I think he's pre-empted that possibility," Nick said. "You've heard about his will?"

"Sure. Who hasn't?"

Nick's shoulders moved as he chuckled. "I mean the clause about Linda?"

"Sure. Everybody's heard. Freddie-boy made sure of that. Maybe it'll hold her in line for a while, maybe it won't. Nobody ain't predicting when it comes to Linda Moreno. She's got what you call . . . temperament."

I said, "Weren't you invited to the party tonight, press agent?"

"Goddamn right I was," Nick said.

"Aren't you going?"

"I went," Nick said. "Now I'm keeping Linda company."

"When you leave?" I said.

"About fifteen minutes ago."

"How was it going?"

"Drinkingly," Nick Wallace said, and rose, and hugged us Broadway fashion, and returned to Linda Moreno's table. Then the ham and eggs arrived.

With hashed brown potatoes.

SEVEN

WHEN I WENT to collect my hat and coat at the checkroom, Joel Barker and Janet Lewis were there ahead of me.

"Hi, private detective," Joel Barker said in his booming voice, grinning slightly.

"Hi, producer," I said.

"Going to Flanders'?" he said.

"On Flanders Field where poppies grow . . ." I said.

"Quite the card," he said, "aren't you?"

"Yep," I said. "Me and Tony Royal."

"Hi, private detective," Janet Lewis said.

"Hi, gorgeous dancer," I said.

She had red hair, and a round face, and round green-eyes, and small boobies, and a muscular posterior, and long and muscular legs. She had been a dancer all her life, had moved from ballet to musical comedy where she had sat them up in their seats yelling bravo in show after show. She should not have been bounding about in the chorus of *Flesh and Fury* as understudy to the star—she should have been the star. Scuttlebutt had it that she had accepted the part in *Flesh and Fury* only through Barker's persuasion, and the persuasions of Barker were no small matters. Joel Barker was a born boss. Put him in a pickle factory and in no time he would be Head Pickle, throw him to the cannibals and the cauldrons would cease cooking until he was Head Head-hunter, let him go for psychiatric treatment and in short order the shrinker would be lying down and Joel would be sitting up. He was a tall, wide-shouldered, thick-bodied, powerful, authoritative man who affected an iron-grey crewcut and a droopy artist-type black bow tie. He had a ruddy, jowly face, beetling eyebrows, and flesh-encased small blue eyes that were bright as a knife. He was a hulk of a man, at least six-feet-four, but he moved easily, like a panther, on strong legs. He was fifty-seven years of age and fighting every day of it. Dear old scuttlebutt had it that if he had persuaded Janet Lewis to downgrade herself to understudy in the show, Linda Moreno was not long for the lights, and Janet would be upgraded to where she belonged: star of *Flesh and Fury*. But there was adverse scuttlebutt to that scuttlebutt. If Janet was Barker's protégée, then Linda was Flanders' protégée

35

and if Barker was a boss, Flanders was a super-boss. No question in the world that Barker was a take-charge guy, and that he knuckled to no man anywhere—except to Freddie Flanders. That was acknowledged. Flanders had been bread-and-butter for Barker for many many years, and Barker had stood like a rock against Flanders' vituperative tongue, and had taken it. If there was a sub-surface contest between Janet and Linda, there was a sub-strata contest between Joel and Freddie—all unspoken, of course: smooth as silk, peaches and cream—but it made for wittily astringent blind items in the gossip columns, and had the bloods of the town all churned up.

Barker retrieved Janet's wrap and hung it about her shoulders. The wrap was a full-length sable coat which Janet could not possibly afford. We got our things, and on the way out, I said, "You kiddies going to Flanders' too?"

"But of course," said Janet Lewis.

"Can I thumb a ride?" I said to Joel.

"Ask her," Joel said. "She's driving."

"Can I thumb a ride?" I said to Janet. "Or should I say may I?"

"Ask him," Janet said. "He's a terribly jealous old tyrant."

"Jealous of him?" Barker chuckled. "Don't make me laugh."

"Now, please," I said, aggrieved.

"Dear wolf," Barker said, "perhaps in ordinary circumstances, a man as young as you, and as pretty, perhaps a tinge would enter into my thinking. But no tinge enters. Wanna know why?"

"I'm bursting," I said.

"Suzy Lyons," he said. "That young lady is on her way to be a star. If you're the boy friend of a star, great demands are made upon you. You're a frazzle of your former self."

"You ought to know," I said.

"Verily," he said, and chuckled again, and shepherded us out into the street where the doorman brought up Janet's Lincoln Continental, and a Lincoln Continental Janet could not afford either.

"Some class," I said to Janet Lewis.

"Thank you," said Joel Barker.

I thought about them, Flanders and Barker, as we drove through the snow; Flanders and Barker, the most successful producing team in the history of the theatre in New York. Freddie was the genius—no trick word—Freddie was the genius, acknowledged, accepted, decorated; an ambulatory landmark, pointed out as frequently as Grant's Tomb or the UN Building—writer (words and music), director and producer of twenty-two very-tip-of-the-top hit shows over the course of the past twenty-five years. (There had been four

flops but even those had paid off as motion picture proper-
ties under the guiding hand of another type of genius—the
word more loosely used: Joel Barker.) Barker was the business
man of the team: all business was in the hands of the sturdy
Barker. They had met thirty years ago when the callow Freddie was bruisingly and unavailingly flinging himself against
the bastions of Tin Pan Alley as a songwriter, and the
slightly more mature Joel was already bored with the routine
of the duties of Certified Public Accountant. Joel had music
in his blood (his father had been a famous concert pianist)
and Freddie had music in his heart, and was overflowing
with it. Freddie played and sang for Joel one night, and Joel
had fallen in love—perhaps "love" is the precise word since
Joel had remained a bachelor for the rest of his life. Joel
had said, "Write a play! You're great! The hell with single
songs! Do a musical!"

And Freddie had said, "Sure, and who'll feed me?"

And Joel had said, "I will."

And Freddie had said, "Can you afford it?"

And Joel had said, "I can. There's an inheritance from
my father."

And Freddie had said, "Sure, and who'll listen? Those
sonsabitches won't listen."

And Joel had said, "Write it! Write it! I know people in
the field, friends of my father! You're great! Write it!
Please! Please!"

It had taken Freddie a year, feeding off Joel, to write
Lady I Love, and it had taken Joel another year to get it
produced—it ran for three years on Broadway, overlapping
Dance Your Head Off, which ran for three years, and overlapped *Sing Me A Sad Song.* Flanders and Barker shows
constantly overlapped one the other, and at this very instant,
there must be twenty Flanders and Barker musicals playing
throughout the world, road companies or revivals.

Quite an enterprise, Flanders and Barker. .

Drinkingly, Nick Wallace had said the party was going,
and drinkingly it must have continued to go. Freddie's town
house was at Sixty-second off Park, four stories of white
granite with many windows, and all the windows were blaz-
ing with light. When we entered we were overwhelmed with
drinking guests who shook hands with us and clapped our
shoulders and kissed us and shook us up. When we got rid of
our outer clothes, other drinking guests shook us and clapped
us and kissed us. There must have been a hundred people,
black-jacketed men and half-naked women. The only sober
ones I noticed were Ethel Flanders, who was Freddie's wife,
and Sara Flanders, who was Freddie's daughter, and Bruce

Lawson, who was Sara's new gentleman friend. I looked about for Suzy Lyons, but there was no Suzy Lyons.

"She hasn't come yet," Ethel Flanders said, smiling sweetly. "May I, in the meantime, lead you to one of the uncrowded bars?"

She led and I followed and even from behind she was still one of the most beautiful women in the world. No exaggerated bumps of figure, no wiggling of the behind, no slithering feline carriage, no pouting of the mouth, no wrinkling of the nose—none of the modern tricks—Ethel Flanders, married to Freddie for twenty-five years, was still one of the most beautiful women in the world. Freddie had plucked her out of his first show, married her, showered her with an effulgence of affection and then, of course, neglected her. But Ethel Flanders was a lady born, and a lady she had remained. In all the frenetic fantastic world of Freddie Flanders, Ethel Flanders remained calm and poised and gentle. She was a statuesque blonde, with a strong-boned face, a fine fair skin, and the clearest, largest, kindliest blue eyes I had ever seen.

"The uncrowded bar," she said as she brought me to it, and to the white-jacketed bartender she said, "Scotch and water for my friend Mr. Chambers. Much Scotch and little water. My friend Mr. Chambers appears singularly sober this evening."

"It's the lack of Suzy Lyons," I said.

"She'll be along," Ethel said. "She's picking up a friend."

"Yeah, I know, at the airport. Who's the friend?"

"I don't know."

"Neither do I."

"Sherry for me," Ethel said to the bartender.

Then Sara Flanders and Bruce Lawson joined us.

"Hi, sleuth," Lawson said.

"Hi, sleuth," I said.

Bruce Lawson was about thirty-three, tall, blond, very handsome and very assured. He had been a photographer who had become an investigator for an insurance company and a pretty good one I had heard. Criminal investigator, he called himself. He was a big guy, the life-guard type, quite brash, and quite unlike any of Sara's boy friends. Sara was rather plain, more like her father, slight of build, with grey eyes and brown hair, and a shrinking, nervous nature. She had met Bruce at a dance at the Ambassador, and it was plain that she was stuck on him. She was nineteen, a brilliant kid already out of college, and most of her swains were the high forehead ones with the heavy-thinking spectacles. I didn't think she was much Bruce's type either, but her father was worth millions, and her mother was an awfully attractive woman and awfully neglected by her husband. I had seen the

38

glances friend Bruce had stolen at Ethel and I had wondered which of the two friends Bruce contemplated taking to bed with him. I did not think he could make it with Sara; it was my opinion that it would require a small charge of dynamite to blast Sara loose from her virginity. On the other hand, I did not think he could make it with the beauteous Ethel either (I must admit I had fought off thoughts in that direction myself). On the third hand, who am I to think upon matters of the hearts or gonads, and of what worth are my opinions in such matters? Let us then say that Bruce Lawson, like sandpaper, rubbed me the wrong way, and since I had no actual reason for that, I remained passive but I stayed out of his way as frequently as I could manage that.

I managed it now by being effusively congenial to the drunks who had finally begun to crowd the uncrowded bar, by wedging through their mass attack upon the bartender, and, lonely for Suzy, drifting, glass in hand, through the many rooms, listening to the latest dirty stories and politely laughing fit to bust. I got a re-fill from another white-jacketed bartender at another bar, drifted again, kissed a few naked feminine shoulders, clapped heartily upon a few masculine shoulders, and was heartily clapped in return. This American habit for the advancement of pleurisy, I thought, would someday be relegated to the limbo of other discarded barbaric customs. In the meantime be wary, I thought, be ready at all times, stay slightly hunched and tensely expectant for the next thunderous blow of shattering good-fellowship. Then I wandered into a little room where Freddie Flanders was declaiming for a group of admirers.

". . . I killed a man today," Freddie was saying.

"Writing a new play?" somebody said.

His admirers were deployed in a wide circle because Freddie was a pacer when he talked, and Freddie was talking. Fabulous Freddie Flanders, with the ever-present darkly amber glass in his hand, talking and pacing and grinning back at his grinning sycophants. Drunk or sober, Freddie Flanders moved with grace. He was a small man, compact and slender as a spur. He was fifty-two years of age, with white hair, a delicate nose, narrow grey eyes, and a small smooth pink face.

"Killed a man today," Freddie said. "A completely new experience."

"For what play?" somebody said.

"When you know you've gotten away with it," Freddie said, "you feel like God."

"Or the devil," somebody said.

"A murder play," somebody else said. "A murder musical. I think it's been done."

"But not like Freddie can do it," somebody said.

"It's a beatific experience," Freddie said. "After you get over your fright, and you know you've done right, and you know they can't catch up with you, it's like coming alive all fresh again, like being reborn."

"Drunk," somebody said. "Drunk as a lord."

"Who said that?" Freddie demanded.

Nobody answered.

"So I'm drunk," Freddie said. "But who wants to take bets, either way?"

"Here comes a quote," somebody said.

"Can a man who's drunk make a quote?" Freddie said.

"No," somebody said.

Freddie waved a hand. "There's the bookcase, ladies and gentlemen. It's full of stuff, Shakespeare and stuff. Go ahead. And don't pick one of the Bard's easy ones."

Somebody went to the bookcase and came back with a book. "This one ain't Shakespeare," that somebody said. "How're you fixed on Moby Dick?"

"Think you can stick me with Melville?" Freddie said. "Try."

"Chapter Five," said the somebody with the book.

Freddie closed his eyes. He wavered for a moment, then drank deeply from his darkly amber glass. "Chapter Five," he said with his eyes closed. "It's entitled 'Breakfast.' Goes like this: 'I quickly followed suit, and descending into the bar-room accosted the grinning landlord very pleasantly. I cherished no malice towards him, though he had been sky-larking with me not a little in the manner of my bedfellow. However, a good laugh is a mighty good thing, and rather too scarce a good thing . . .' "

"Wow," said somebody looking over the shoulder of the somebody holding the open book. "This guy's a wizard. Absolutely."

I wandered out, seeking Suzy. No question Fabulous Freddie Flanders was fabulous, drunk or sober, although, upon thought, I had never seen him precisely sober. Freddie had the reputation of being a drinking man, and Freddie lived up to his reputation.

And then I saw Suzy Lyons.

She came in with a sunburnt girl. The sunburnt girl had a tiny upturned nose, wide black upturned eyes, and black swirling short-cut hair. Sara hurried to them, greeted them and took their coats. Suzy was still wearing her last change from the show. It was an off-the-shoulder dress, slit to the navel, cinched at the waist, and it had a flaring transparent skirt. Suzy could carry it—leave it to Suzy. Suzy could be wearing a fig-leaf and regally stare down all starers. The sunburnt girl had a trim figure in a formfitting lavender suit.

Her blouse and accessories were black and she wore black spike-heeled pumps and tight black nylons. She had lovely calves.

But I had no eyes for lavender figures or lovely calves.

I had eyes for Suzy Lyons.

EIGHT

Suzy Lyons had to be seen to be believed. Suzy Lyons was America's answer to sizzling Italian movie stars, incandescent French movie stars, sulphurous Spanish movie stars, and aphrodisiac Greek movie stars. Since the measure of talent for the wide screen seems to be the measurement of the bosom (and other vital areas), Suzy was as sought after by the movie moguls as the fox is sought after by the hounds. The proportions of Suzy's vital areas could set fire to asbestos. The protuberance of Suzy's mammary glands would send the latest Italian fireball to hide behind a cow's udder in shame—yet on Suzy every item appeared discreetly proportionate. Rubens would have painted her. Epstein would have sculpted her. Casanova would have devoured her. Don Quixote would have tilted at her. I adored her.

Suzy Lyons had eyes like sky, hair like sun, skin like the softest of clouds—all of which goes to make up a good part of heaven. Suzy Lyons was a good part of heaven. She was also a good part of hell. Suzy Lyons had lips that glistened like a fresh-minted coin, a smile that gleamed like ivory, and legs that out-marlened the utmost of Dietrich. The motion picture companies stood in line, hat in hand, and each hat brimming with gold, waiting for Suzy to sign on the dotted line for one picture a year at two hundred thousand per picture, but Suzy was not having any—not yet. Suzy was a dancer, a singer, an actress, in love with her career, and on her way up. She had come out of dramatic school into a musical called *Bugaboo* where she had been upped from the chorus to a featured role. Her second show had been *Hooray for Hannah* where she had been third lead. Her third show was *Flesh and Fury* where she was second lead. Right now Shaw and Hammerlock were doing a musical specially conceived for Suzy, and she would be a star. After that, she promised, she might be ready for the movies.

Suzy was twenty-three, but ageless. Suzy was born with an old head. Suzy wanted absolutely no part of marriage but Suzy was not averse to male attention. So I fit, but I had no illusions. Neither did she. Right now we were very much in love, but Suzy was not going to stop with me, and I was not going to stop with Suzy. We were of similar tempera-

41

ment—about as permanent as quicksilver—but right now we were very much in love.

She saw me and she called out, "Hi, lover. Buy me a drink, won't you? I'm frozen."

I bought her a couple of drinks. I bought myself a couple of drinks too. Then I led her upstairs and I sat her down in a corner of a quiet room and we clinked glasses and sipped and I ate her up in silence. So she said, "Why're you worried, lover?"

"Me? Worried?"

"You. Worried."

"I'm never worried when I'm with you, sweetie."

"Shove it, sweetie. What's bothering you?"

"It shows?" I said.

"Written all over you," she said. "Tell Mama."

"I've got a client," I said.

"Oh, I'm real glad for you," she said.

"Stop with the jibes," I said. "His name is Duff. Ever hear the name Duff?"

She pursed her lips like a kiss. "Mmm, I think so."

"Katy Duff?"

"Mmm, I think so."

"Good friend of yours?"

"Uh huh."

"She's with the show?"

"Uh huh."

"Cute?"

"Uh huh."

"So how come I never met her?"

She kissed my ear. She said at my ear, "You think I'm nuts, lover? I keep you away from the cute ones."

"Her father's paid me a thousand bucks to find out a little bit about her. Will you help?"

"For you to earn a thousand bucks—sure I'll help."

We clinked glasses again and sipped. "She took a month's leave of absence," I said. "She didn't tell her old man."

"Maybe she didn't want her old man to know."

"Why not?"

"I really don't know. But it's not unusual. Girls have secrets from their parents. Happens all the time. Even boys have secrets from their parents. I'm real bright, eh, lover?"

"A month's leave of absence," I said. "Vacation?"

"I think so."

"You know where she went?"

"Yep."

"Where?"

"Havana."

That threw me. "Havana?" I said.

"What's wrong with Havana?" she said.

"Sweetie," I said, "something's cockeyed. Papa got letters from her. They were all postmarked New York."

"Oh, I can explain that," she said. "Only for your thousand dollars. I like it when you earn fees."

"Explain," I said.

"Katy wrote some letters. She gave them to me. I was to mail one of them each Thursday. I mailed one each Thursday. Like that, I imagine, Papa got letters from her all postmarked New York."

"Did she tell you why?" I said.

"Nope."

"Didn't you ask her?"

"Nope. I don't pry. If she'd have wanted to tell me, she'd have told me."

I sat back and I sipped Scotch. I lit a cigarette and I dragged hard. "Cute?" I said. "Real cute?"

"Real cute," she said.

"And young?"

"Real cute and young."

"Then Freddie must have moved in."

"You know Freddie."

"Did he?"

"I don't know," she said. "She's a close-mouthed kid, and I don't pry. He took her out, gave her a real big play when she first joined the show. But you know Freddie. He tires easily. And there was Linda. You know Freddie. He'll grab a new chick for kicks, give her a fast fling, then give her the fast boot, and back to whoever's his steady at the moment. Linda's his steady at the moment."

"It's been a long moment."

"Maybe she's got a lot on the ball."

"Nuts," I said. I finished my drink, took hers and lapped at that. "What about Allan Sylvester?" I said.

"Boy, you know everything, don't you?"

"Far from it," I said. "What about Sylvester?"

"That one I warned her about."

"Did she listen?"

"Who listens?" she said. "He's a charmer, that son of a bitch. She flipped for him."

"When'd she meet him?"

"A couple of months ago. I introduced them."

"Real jolly. First you introduce them, then you warn her."

"No, it wasn't like that," she said. "There was a party after the show a couple of months ago. He was there. He came over and asked to meet her. What could I do? I introduced them. But that's all. I tried to talk her out of him fast, but she wasn't buying. She flipped. It happens."

43

"All the time, with that guy."

"Well, it happened with her. Of course, he turned on the charm real heavy. Maybe he was stuck on her too."

"Did she give him a key?"

"What? What's that?"

"A key. For 78th Street."

"Boy, you know everything, don't you?"

"Why? Because I know where she lives? Did she give him a key?"

"Peter, my boy, I wouldn't tell you that even if I knew. Not even to earn you your thousand bucks."

"Do you know?"

"As a matter of fact, I don't," she said. "But as long as you're that interested, why don't you ask her? Or don't you have the nerve?"

"I've got the nerve, love-bird. Only it'd be kind of tough to spring that over the telephone. I'd get hung up on, period."

"Telephone?"

"Havana. Remember? You're the one who told me."

"Oh, she's back."

"When was this?"

"Tonight."

"You're kidding."

"I wouldn't kid you, sweetie. Never. She's why I went out to the airport. I picked her up myself."

"Where is she?"

"Here."

"No."

"You saw me come in with her. The cute brunette with the turned-up nose."

NINE

"Baby," I said, "I want to talk to her."

"Baby," she said, "only if it's business."

"Baby," I said, "it's business."

She stood up and she stretched. I gulped. When Suzy Lyons stands and stretches, you gulp. If you don't, you're a eunuch. "Baby," I said, "for you to be jealous, you're out of your mind."

"So I'm out of my mind," she said. "If it's business, I'll get her for you. But it had better be business, kiddo."

"It's business," I said.

"I'll get her," she said.

"Hold it," I said.

"What?" she said.

"Two things," I said. "First, I'm going to have to get out of here. And second, I'm going to take her with me."

44

"What the hell are you talking about?" she said.

"Her father's here in town. He's terribly worried about her. It's part of my job to get her to him."

"If it's part of your job," she said. "And after that?"

"Whatever you say."

"Maybe I don't know about Allan Sylvester, but I know about you."

"Meaning?"

"You've got a key that doesn't open your own door, remember?"

"I remember," I said.

"I'll see you later," she said.

"Just a minute."

"What?"

"Don't mention anything to her. Papa doesn't want her to know he's been checking on her."

"I dig," she said.

"Thanks," I said.

"See you later," she said.

"I dig," I said.

She went off and I watched her go and I thought about how lucky I was, and when she came back with Katy Duff, I was still thinking about how lucky I was, and drooling slightly in anticipation of a command performance, and I had to shift gears to get my mind back to Katy Duff.

"Katy Duff," Suzy said. "Peter Chambers. Hands off, Katy. He's mine. All mine. He'd better be. See you later," she said and went away.

Katy sat down beside me. "I love her," Katy said. She had a throaty voice, sexy, and she knew it, and she used it. She was better looking from up close than from a distance. Her black eyes were deep and liquid and the planes of her face all pointed upward: high cheekbones, upturned nose and upturned corners at the edges of her eyes. But she wore the usual Mata Hari mask of all the young ones. Simply, they think they have secrets that no one else ever heard of. How goddamned wrong they are. But I liked it. I liked the fact that she wore the weary mask of all the young ones. I was working now, working at my business, and cracking that world-weary mask of nothingness would help me learn what I wanted to know.

"You're lovely," I said.

"Thank you," she said. She was accustomed to that. Her face was as fathomless as a clock without hands.

"Your father's in town," I said.

"Gee, good!" The eyes lit up with pleasure, but all the secrets stayed in the face.

"I'm to bring you to him," I said.

"Well, let's go," she said.

"Honey," I said, "I've been around."

"So?"

"So I'm on your side."

"I beg your pardon?"

"Maybe I'm not supposed to tell you, but I'm telling you anyway. He wants to talk to you—about Allan Sylvester."

The eyes seemed to recede. They grew almost crafty. She was not fighting me. She was fighting the old man. If he's going to try to stick his nose into my business, the eyes said, he's going to get that nose snapped off. I don't stick my nose into his private affairs—let him keep his nose out of mine. He's my father, okay he's my father, but I'm all grown-up, and I have a private life, and unless I want him to enter that private life, he and anyone else had better stay out of that private life. A grown-up girl has rights, goddamn it, I'm even grown-up enough to feel the cuss-words without terror.

"Thanks," she said. "Thanks for the warning. You're a good guy. You'd have to be a good guy, the way Suzy feels about you. She's tops."

"About Allan Sylvester," I said.

"Let's go see Dad," she said.

"It's not that he has any objection," I said.

"Pardon?" she said and the eyes blinked but the face was wood.

"It's something nobody knows about, except your Dad, and me, and now you."

"About Allan? What?"

"He's dead."

"Dead!"

"He was found dead. In your apartment. We found him, your old man and I. Dead. Allan Sylvester. In your apartment."

First she looked at me, almost studying me, all grown-up. And then it hit her. She saw I was telling the truth. And then the face came apart, like the face of a child whose lollipop was brutally pulled from her mouth. Shock tore her face apart. The eyes squinted, tears springing. The mouth quivered. The planes of the face were marred. Suddenly, beneath all the sophisticated make-up, a little girl peered up at me, pitifully. I wanted to take her in my arms, and nestle that face against my shoulder, and stroke her hair. The stupid little grown-up mask disintegrated and the agony was as patent as a knife drawing blood.

Whatever else might happen, I was all the way with Edward Duff. Katy Duff was innocent of Allan Sylvester, alive or dead. Whatever Edward Duff had done to shield this stricken child, I approved. More, I admired his goddamned nerve.

I took her face in my hands and kissed her forehead.

"Honey," I said. "Let's go talk to your father."

46

TEN

I CALLED HIM before we came there, and when we arrived he was sleepy-eyed but stalwart in creased black pants and a brave white shirt. His daughter fled from me and he enclasped her and his face over her shoulder beseeched me to leave them to their private talk.

I left without a word.

I went where I had been bidden.

I was an inadequate lover. I talked, I remember, sobbingly. I remember going away, to a bottle, and drinking from the bottle. I talked, violating the ethics of my profession. I pleaded that it be confidential and I knew that my plea would be honored. I wept, perhaps for my own sins, and I was comforted. She held me like a mother, and kissed the top of my head, and patted my body tenderly.

I remember lurching in my sleep and groaning.

And I remember tears on my face, not my own.

ELEVEN

IN THE MORNING, I went home wearing my tuxedo and my hangover. I shed the tuxedo and tried to shed the hangover with burp-bromo and vitamin pills. I stripped and went to the stall shower and stalled for a long time in the stall shower, occasionally rubbing soap along the crevices of my body. I kept the water hot and I steamed. It helped. Then I turned the water to cold, in the dictates of the most recent health fad (and there are constantly so many, are there not?), and I shivered, and gasped, and got the hell out of there. Maybe that helped too. I dried down and grabbed a huge shot of the hair-of-the-dog—and it all added up to some sort of succor. I had a large appetite and a small headache. I squeezed oranges, beat up eggs and laid out the bacon.

I called down for the *Times* and the *News*.

Over breakfast, I sopped up current events.

The *Times* had nothing except domestic politics, international foment, space-talk about launchings and rockets, a favorable book review, and, of course, an unfavorable theatre review. The *News* had it on Page Three: ANOTHER GANGLAND KILLING IN BRONX. It went on to tell about Allan Sylvester, his picturesque background and his present estate. His present estate was "dead, with a bullet in his heart, stripped of all identification, and, in usual gangland fashion, thrown out into the street. A typical gangland killing of a typical minor gangland figure . . ."

I ate my breakfast.

I called the office. There were no messages for me.

Then I did the one chore that daily made me sad that I was a bachelor—I washed the dishes. I also cleaned up. Then I shaved, dressed, and went to see my friend Detective-lieutenant Louis Parker of Homicide. I thought about using the car but decided, of course, upon a taxi. In New York you use your car as though it had a trailer attached—only for long trips.

Who needs the ulcer?

I took a cab.

Louis Parker, plump as a dumpling but hard as a keg, was a short man with bristling black hair, strong teeth, a world-weary attitude, and an honorable soul. His cigar, as I sat down on the other side of his desk, was unlit but wedged at a peculiar angle in his mouth: it looked sardonic. A copy of the *News* was spread before him, open at Page Three.

"Hi, dick," he said. "How goes Romeo?"

"Who's Romeo?" I said.

"You're Romeo," he said. "Between you and me, I think it's a sickness."

"The sickness," I said, "is that everybody talks about sicknesses these days. Freud is spinning."

"You're a latent homosexual," he said. "You've got a Don Juan complex."

"Kiss my ass," I said.

"That's what I mean," he said. "Unconsciously, you'd like that."

"I can tell you where else to kiss me," I said.

"Don't get riled," he said. "I'm kidding."

"Where'd you learn this kind of kidding?"

The cigar shifted to another angle. Sheepish. "I'm being analyzed," he said.

"By whom?" I said.

"By whom the hell do you think?" he said. "An analyst."

"You?" I said. "You're the most solid son of a bitch I've ever met."

"For kicks," he said.

"Analysis for kicks?" I said. "That's a new one."

"I'm a thoroughgoing cop," he said. "Every slob is talking a brand new kind of a lingo, as I'm learning first hand. The next marijuana-punk I nab who stuck a knife into his mother, I want to know what he means when he tells me it's got to do with Oedipus. So what brings you, laddie, though I'm always glad to see you?"

"Allan Sylvester," I said.

48

He lit the cigar. He cocked it at a new angle. Interested. "Which side are you on, laddie?"

"Your side," I said.

"I take your word," he said. He touched the *News.* "See the papers?"

"Gangland killing," I said.

"Gangland my Oedipus," he said. "What do you know about this?"

"Nothing," I lied. "That's why I'm here."

"What's your interest?"

"The same as yours, Louie."

"You said that before, laddie. Do you have a client?"

"Yes."

"Can you tell me?"

"No."

"What does your client want?"

"Wants that your books are closed on this—as a gangland killing."

"They're wide open, laddie."

"Why?" I said.

He puffed on his cigar, rolled it around in his mouth, and his eyes stayed on my face as though there were something crawling on it. "Your client interested in who killed him?"

"Yes."

"You working on that?"

"Yes, Louie."

"We pool our stuff, laddie?"

"Absolutely, Louie. We've worked together before, I hope we'll work together again. I've never crossed you, have I?"

"No sir, you haven't." He sighed. "I wish, sometimes, I could have the free hand you have. I mean, no regulations. I mean your . . . er . . . unorthodox methods."

"You do all right, Louie."

"I'm bound to the use of legal means. You're not—that is, you get away with as much as you *can* get away with."

"It's a good combination, Papa. In the end, whatever I come up with, I turn over to you. And I don't ask for any credit, do I?"

He smiled around the cigar. "But you ask for favors, don't you, kid?"

"It's fair trade, isn't it?"

"Yes," he said as he sighed again, "I suppose it is. What do you want?"

"Same as my client. I want it to be a gangland killing."

"Well, it's not!" He bumped a stubby finger at the newspaper in front of him. "Usual gangland fashion. Typical gangland killing. Bull," he said.

"Why?" I said.

He squinted over the cigar. "We got a deal? We're working on the same thing from opposite ends?"

"Absolutely," I said.

"Okay," he said and he grunted. "First off, one bullet in the heart. That's no ride-job. A ride-job is three four slugs in the back of the head, the neck."

"It didn't have to be a ride. Suppose he got it right there, on the street."

"Same answer. Did you ever hear of a pro job with just one lousy little slug? Never. Not on a dark and lonely street, kiddo. Plus I even got a topper for that."

"Shoot, pal."

"The one slug—the one slug that killed him—was a twenty-two."

"A twenty-two?" I said.

"Ever hear of a professional job with a twenty-two?"

"No, sir," I said.

"See what I mean?"

"Yes, sir," I said.

"That's all we got, laddie, but we do have one wonderful little advantage that we don't usually have." He tapped the newspaper again. "Because Sylvester was who he was, and the way he was found—the press says 'typical gangland killing of a typical minor gangland figure' which takes the pressure off us. A mob rub-out, they don't expect us to clean it up, and they don't care. Vermin exterminating vermin, they like it. It's a nice advantage. No pressure, no pushing-around, no criticism. Tomorrow, it's yesterday's news. There'll be no ringing editorial, no box on the front page, no digs at the dumb cops. It's nice when there's no pressure."

"Real great," I said and I got up.

"But we'll be working on it, laddie."

"So will I."

"And we'll be hearing from you?"

"You bet," I said.

"Damn right I bet." He smiled and his eyes crinkled benignly.

The way he said it, it did not sound like a threat. It was.

From the hot booth of a cool saloon I called the New York office of Duff, Sherman and Becker and asked for Mr. Duff. After the normal sequence of telephonic clickings a male voice poured through the wire with enough syrup to douse hotcakes. "Not in," he purred. "Mr. Duff, actually, isn't at this office official, until December One actually. On the other hand, if you wish to leave a name and number, I'm certain that Mr. Duff shall be in touch with you. Actually—

50

I hung up. It was early. The cool saloon was empty. The bartender looked lonely. I bought a shot for me and a shot for him, the best. Before he got his breath to begin the conversation on politics, the weather, traffic or dames, I paid him and went to the Waldorf.

Duff still had egg on his mouth but his eyes looked miserable.

"Join me in breakfast," he said.

"I ate," I said.

"A drink?"

"I'm on the wagon," I said. I looked around. "Where's Katy?"

"Katy?" he said. "I . . . er . . . she . . ."

He went to the breakfast nook and I chugged after him like I was playing choo-choo train. He sat down to his eggs and I sat down to contemplating him. The guy looked like death on a scooter. The healthy California tan had diminished to a moldy beige, the flesh of his face sagged in lumpy pouches and the lines from nostrils to mouth-edge were deeper than the cleavage of the newest television songbird.

I let him eat.

Then I said, "Where's Katy?"

"She . . . uh . . . she's quit the show." He dabbed at his lips with a napkin. He used the same napkin to dab at his forehead where the perspiration was showing.

"Retired?" I said.

"At least temporarily," he said.

I lit a cigarette. "You've gotten her out of town, haven't you?"

"Yes."

"I'm going to the cops," I said.

He pushed back and stood up. "Please," he said. "Please help me."

"Nuts," I said. "Are we back on that routine?"

"She had nothing to do with his murder."

"How do you know?"

"She was in Havana."

"How do you know?"

"She told me."

"What else did she tell you?"

"She came back last night. You know all about that. Suzy picked her up at the airport. You know all about that. Well, if she was in Havana, then she couldn't have been here. And if she wasn't here, she couldn't have killed him. And if she didn't kill him, why should we mix her into this?"

"Where is she?"

"On the plane to California."

"She going to stay there?"

"No. I've arranged for a quick stay, and then she's going to Honolulu."

51

"Pretty soft for Katy."

"Please. Don't say that."

"Why not, Mr. Duff?"

"That child is cured. She's been through . . . through hell. I can't let more happen to her. Please. Please try to understand."

"I don't know what the hell you're talking about, Mr. Duff."

He looked like he was going to fall. He reached back and eased himself into the chair. I donated a cigarette and lit it for him. He smoked grimly and topped it with cold coffee. "She was like a little child here last night," he said. "Like a little child who had tried playing at grown-up and had found it too much for her. She broke down completely. Let's give her a chance. Please."

"She was in love with this Sylvester?" I said.

"Infatuated would be a better word."

"And she broke up because he was knocked off?"

"More. More than that. She's been through hell."

"You said that, Mr. Duff."

"I'm saying it again." He pulled on the cigarette and swallowed 'smoke. "She'll be good from now on, I know that. She'll go to college, and she'll study dramatics, and she'll probably turn out to be a fine actress. Let's give her a chance."

"What about the bit you pulled with Sylvester?"

"I'm glad I did it."

"Great. But what about it?"

"She didn't kill him."

"But what about it?"

"Whatever happened there, she had nothing to do with it. And what I did, kept her clear of it."

"Look," I said. "A man is dead. A louse, I admit. But a man is dead, and we can't set ourselves up as God. We've frigged up an investigation. We've got the papers talking about a gang-ride killing. You did a great job for your daughter, Mr. Duff, but what have you done for the old cornball deal of the forces of law and order?"

"I'll go to them. I'll tell them."

"When?"

"When it dies down a bit. When it's not hot copy. When she won't be important to it any more."

"Now, look, I don't want to be—"

"But she wasn't here! She was in Havana!"

"How do you know?"

"She told me."

"That's not proof, Mr. Duff—that she told you. What else did she tell you?"

"Pardon?"

"What about that month's leave of absence? What about those phony letters?"

He put the point of the cigarette into the coffee, let it hiss to death and laid it into the saucer. "She . . . er . . . she was tired. She wasn't used to the climate. She . . . er . . . she needed a rest, needed some sunshine. The reason for the letters is that she didn't wish to worry me."

It was so obvious, it was embarrassing.

"You're lying," I said, "and it figures one of two ways. Either, purely, you're lying, because you want to cover up, or, Katy lied to you, and, with the full knowledge that she was lying, you're passing her lies along to me." The filmy eyes in the sagging handsome face pleaded with me, but they were as stubborn as an unhinged zipper. "Okay," I said. "I'm old enough to know that when you beat your head against a stone wall it bounces back bloody on you. A papa standing protective in front of a daughter is a stone wall. I'm not beating my head."

Simply he said, "Thank you."

"Then let's get practical," I said.

"Pardon?" he said.

"Cops," I said.

"Pardon?" he said.

"You're trying to keep her clear of it," I said. "You've sent her away. You want to keep her away until it blows over. It won't blow over unless they find his murderer—or, for you and your family, it won't blow over until you go to the cops and fess up your end of it. That she told you she was in Havana isn't enough. It's what she told you. That's hearsay, that's not proof. Perhaps if we have proof, actual proof, we won't have to drag her into it, personally."

"Yes, yes," he said eagerly. "I see. What do you suggest?"

"Proof."

"Yes, but I mean—"

"She been in Havana the entire month?"

"Yes."

"Where did she stay?"

"She was a house guest."

"Fine," I said. "Whose house guest?"

"Millay," he said. "Dee Dunstan Millay. Mr. and Mrs. Dee Dunstan Millay."

"Dee Dunstan Millay?"

"You know him?"

"Slightly." Now I was lying. I knew Dee Dunstan Millay more than slightly. "Okay, let's check it out with them."

"I beg your pardon?"

"Look, Daddy. We're trying to establish a proper alibi

53

for daughter. If she was a house guest in Havana, let's check it out with her hosts. That's what I mean by proof, Daddy."

"Yes, I see. All right. Call them." He gestured to the phone.

"That would be more hearsay, Daddy. That would be me, some time in the future, telling the cops that I talked with the Millays and that they told me what Katy told you. No good. I want to get that stuff down on affidavits, signed, sealed and sworn. That would keep them from changing their minds in case they wanted to change their minds some time in the future, if you know what I mean. If you want it good, Daddy, then you want it airtight. You're banker enough to know that, aren't you?"

He was fighting a battle with himself and one of him was bound to lose. Reluctance was as thick on his face as pancake makeup on a teenager, but his eyes suddenly glowed with a banker's glow. A pragmatic mind was in combat with a paternal heart: you could tell that the heart wanted me to stay right here in New York but you could also tell that the mind proclaimed that I was talking sense.

"Would you go down there?" he said timidly.

"If you pay the expenses," I said.

"You'll be . . . discreet?"

"Daddy-o, since I've met you I've been more discreet than the madame of a whorehouse in Maine."

The battle was over. "Will you go at once?" he said.

"As at-once as you can arrange it for me."

"That's easy," he said and went to the phone and called the New York office of Duff, Sherman and Becker. He was brisk and efficient on the phone, and while he waited I brought him a new cigarette and lit it for him, and then I prowled the apartment, and then he talked some more on the phone, and then he hung up and he said, "There's a flight at six o'clock this evening. Your tickets will be waiting at the airport. Good luck, Mr. Chambers."

"Happy landings," I said.

TWELVE

THE BUZZER OF Suzy's apartment returned an echo but no answer. I could have used my key but that might have been an intrusion. I went downstairs and called her on the telephone. After four rings, Service answered. Service, this trip, was a Southern accent with high-pitched resonance. "Miss Lyons's residence," Service intoned.

"Miss Lyons," I said meekly.

"Not at home, suh. Who is a-calling, please?"

54

"Mr. Chambers, but it makes no matter, sweet-bud."

"Oh, Mr. Chambers, there is a message if a Mr. Chambers calls."

"Mr. Chambers is a-calling, Daisy-belle. All of him."

"Miss Lyons is a-waiting you at Royal House, suh. For lunch."

"The colonel salutes you, Scarlett me love. From the very pit of his stomach."

"Oh I remember you." She giggled. "You're the crazy Sherlock character. How've you all been? I've been out with them crazy flu germs, virus."

"All of me's been real swell, dam-yankee."

"Getting drunk in the afternoon ain't fittin'," she said.

"This is Service?" I said.

"This is Gwendolyn," she said. "You remember me, Sherlock. You and me got drunk in the afternoon one afternoon."

"Hold that Confederate tongue," I said. "That was early in my acquaintance with Miss Lyons, you-all. We're engaged to be getting all-fired married, me and Missy."

"Well, good luck," she said.

"And a sea-green mint-Julep to you," I said, "but how's about a rain-check for some future afternoon gymnastics, just in case?"

"Just in case what?" she said.

"Just in case the bottom falls out of Missy."

"You're the nutsiest," she said. "But you just call in case that bottom drops."

"I've got fond recollections," I said, "you-all."

"Maybe the bottom's already fallen, lovey-pie," she said.

"How's that?" I said.

"A Mr. Duff's been banging the phone," she said with a meow. "Called four times."

"Fluff your duff," I said.

"Pardon, Sugar?" she said.

"You're the nutsiest," I said and hung up.

Poor Duff had a lingering headache about Katy, I thought, as I breasted the November wind toward Royal House. Poor Duff, trying to play it cool with me, was anxious for further returns from Suzy. Poor old Duff had been holding out on me, I thought, as I crunched through snow, but poor old Duff had every right to keep the personal things about Katy personal to him and Katy. He would not learn much from Suzy, but he would have to admire her. Duff admired people who were discreet. Suzy was discreet.

"You're discreet," I said to Suzy as I wedged in beside her at Royal House.

"Ain't nuthin if not," Suzy said batting her magnificent eyes at me. "Where the hell you been? I've been calling and calling."

"And Mr. Duff's been calling and calling."

"I know. I'm not calling back."

"But why?" I said.

"The kid called me and told me she was flying home. So what can I say to Mr. Duff? Something like hello?"

"Something like," I said. "What's that sitting in front of you?"

"A stinger."

"A stinger is lunch?" I said.

"I'm not having lunch," she said. "I'm waiting for you."

"So now we have lunch?"

"Not here," she said. "Wave to Freddie."

Freddie was at a table with Linda, Nick Wallace and Tony Royal. Freddie was waving at me, and I waved back. Linda was saying, and it carried all the way to us: ". . . cruelty is part of your make-up, Freddie. You can't help yourself."

Freddie stopped waving and returned to Linda. "If I can't help myself, my raven-haired one, why make a point of it?" And he said to Nick Wallace, "Can't you keep her in line, young fella?"

At their favorite table, Joel Barker and Janet Lewis pretended to hear and see nothing, except themselves.

"Let's blow," Suzy said.

"Where we going?" I said.

"Ethel made lunch with her own hands. We're invited."

"I'm going to Havana," I said.

"Sure," Suzy said, "but let's first have lunch that Ethel made with her own hands."

"So finish the stinger," I said. "I take it it's paid for."

"It's paid for," she said and finished it. "And just to get ourselves straightened out, lover, I know where you got the information about Duff calling me, and other information you pick up now and then. You've laid that Southern-fried chicken at Service and she's trying to work out a repeat performance. I wouldn't if I were you."

"Don't be silly," I said.

"I'm not silly," she said. "I'm the nutsiest."

"I've got to go to Havana," I said.

"Let's first go eat Ethel's lunch," she said. "And remember about that cornpone dish. It's not just that I'm jealous; simply it's bad for my reputation if that chick and I are playing catch with the same pitcher. We're not supposed to be in the same league."

On our way out, I stopped at Freddie's table. A weird hunch had been bouncing in my mind like the white ball of a community sing. I played my hunch because my hunch had a glint of reason. "Freddie," I said, "did you read about that gangland killing in Bronx?"

"What the hell?" he said looking up from a Scotch mist.

"Allan Sylvester," I said.

"Who he?"

Freddie was so sternly casual, it delighted me.

"You remember that punk," Suzy said.

"Allan Sylvester?" Freddie pleated his forehead.

"Ask me sometime," I said, "how come he was found in the Bronx."

"I didn't know that you had ever heard of the Bronx," Freddie said but his narrow grey eyes were very narrow and the flush of his face was not all Scotch. I was so delighted I was all ready to break out into a community sing of my own.

"I'm going to Havana," I said with insouciance.

"Why don't you also go and drop dead," Freddie said.

"And then get transported to the Bronx," I said.

"You ought to get rid of this joker, Suzy," Freddie said. "He's rather a blight."

"A blight for sore eyes," Suzy said.

"Oh no," Freddie said. "Why don't you both go drop dead in the Bronx?"

"Beloved," I said. "Like that how'll we get transported?"

"Go away," Freddie said. "But come back sometime."

"I accept," I said and took Suzy by the arm and led her to the checkroom. Freddie and I had a compact. Freddie was a bright man. Freddie was a genius. At that moment I felt that maybe I was a genius.

"What's with the needle for Freddie?" Suzy said. "You look like you're going to break into song."

"Community song," I said.

"What?" Suzy said.

"Let's go eat," I said, "Ethel's handmade lunch."

Ethel was wearing a tight blue dress without a girdle and Bruce Lawson's eyes reacted to every shimmer. The lunch was Sara and Bruce and Ethel and Suzy and me, and the lunch was French style, and everybody said it was delicious, but I picked like a sparrow in the park.

"Something wrong?" Ethel asked me in a soft worried tone.

"He's going to Havana," Suzy said. "Personally, I think he's switched to reefers."

I stood up and I said, "I've got to pack a few nonsense things, I suppose. Wanna help, Sue?"

"That what they call it now?" Bruce Lawson said brightly.

I had an impulse to pull him up by his Windsor knot and belt him but I restrained the impulse. "Beautiful lunch," I said to Ethel, "and I apologize. Blame it on Havana."

"What's so gosh-awful about Havana?" Sara piped.

"Nothing except I gotta go," I said.

57

"If he's gotta go, he's gotta go," Suzy said. "And I may as well help him pack his few nonsense things." She patted Bruce's blond head but she patted it stiff-palm. "And that *is* what they call it now, Buster," she said.

At my apartment, I threw in a lightweight suit and a change of diapers, and I was packed.

"You're not going for long," Suzy said, "are you?"

"A day or two."

"What time's the plane?"

"Six."

"So what's all the rush?"

"I want to talk to you."

"That's all?"

"First, I want to talk to you."

"I'll take second," she said, blithe and bright, but she was not feeling it. Suzy was a modern young lady who had to act modern. Any show of emotion, unless in bed, was against the rules. You play the game according to the rules of the generation into which you have been born. Suzy's generation, the generation of the ballistic missile, was blithe and bright and brittle be it the moment of identifying a suicide on a slab in the morgue.

I lay out on the couch.

She came to me and knelt and took my head to her bosom. "Stinking world," she said.

"I love you," I said.

"You were crazy last night," she said.

"Stinking world," I said. "I told you the whole bit, didn't I?"

"The whole bit," she said.

"I'll tell you more," I said.

I told her about today: Parker and Duff.

"So why the needle to Freddie?" she said.

I sat up. "Yesterday, at the party, he was sounding off about murdering a man who was right for murdering."

"Oh, you know Freddie. He was creating. Out loud."

"You say creating. I say boasting. You know Freddie. I know Freddie. It could be either, couldn't it?"

"Yes, but my way—"

"Hold it, honey."

"I'm holding, honey."

"Let's try to add up a couple of items."

"Add away, lover boy."

"He must have had a thing with Katy, a sweet young thing right out of the sticks and into his show. Yes?"

She stiffened. "I don't know."

"But it puts him close to Katy, no?"

"Yes."

58

"Plus he knows Sylvester which he kind of tried to deny before, right?"

"Right."

"Plus Katy went to Dee Dunstan Millay, right?"

"Right."

"Dee and Freddie, they're close like a couple of crossed fingers, right?"

"Yes, right."

"Kind of has Freddie swinging in the middle. No?"

"Kind of has him touching each point here and there," she said. "I don't know about the swinging."

I kissed her and then I backed off. "What glued it together for me, at least for my hunch, was something you once told me."

"About what?"

"About Freddie."

"What about Freddie?"

"Freddie owns a gun, doesn't he? You told me."

"Yes," she said slowly and her big eyes became bigger. "I remember."

"You told me the calibre, remember?"

"I remember."

"Say it," I said at her big blue eyes. "What the hell are you fighting?"

"It could be coincidence, couldn't it?"

"Of course it could be. Now say it."

"No. You say it. Freddie's been good to me. Freddie's crazy. There are people who say he's the worst. Maybe. Maybe I've seen the good side of him. Even the worst has a good side. You say it, Peter."

"Freddie Flanders owns a gun. It's a tight little job. It's a twenty-two. I'm saying it. You once told it to me, but right now I'm saying it."

She took my head to her bosom. It was sudden. It upset my equilibrium. I rolled off the couch. I put my arms around her and held her. We lay like that, enclasped, like two frightened children, on the floor.

THIRTEEN

THE PLANE DRONED and I dozed and I marshalled my facts on Dee Dunstan Millay. Dee Dunstan was a snappy chap, crowding fifty, whose psyche contained more twists than a girlie show. Dee Dunstan was an obsession-ridden, compulsive-driven, AC-DC, bilateral personality, but Dee Dunstan was entitled to a splintered psyche because Dee Dunstan was an artist. Dee Dunstan was probably the greatest arranger of our time, a musician and a composer of note, and Freddie Flanders had grabbed him early and had held on to him for a long time. For twelve years, Dee Dunstan had been head man in the pit for every Flanders and Barker show, orchestra leader, arranger and musical director. Aside from his salary, and because of his unbounded confidence in Freddie and himself, he had invested heavily in each of Freddie's shows and he had waxed fat and frivolous therefrom. He had waxed fatter after he had met Mimi Ressip.

Mimi Lydia Ressip had been a lady stockbroker with a good head on her shoulders. She had already begun, at the time Dee Dunstan met her, to pour too much brandy into that good head on her shoulders, but it had not yet affected her financial judgment. Mimi was a descendant of a gone-broke high-society family: a tall, poised, cultured woman with broad shoulders, a flat chest and a mannish stride. Her investments on Dee Dunstan's behalf had netted him a comfortable capital-gains fortune of well over a million bucks. It had also netted him a drinking companion who appreciated music and appreciated the fact that Dee Dunstan had never made a pass at her and never would. Mimi did not desire passes. She was ten years older than Dee Dunstan, tired, and ready to abandon herself to judicious imbibing, but on a twenty-four hour schedule. She had full knowledge that as to her own sex, Dee Dunstan's infrequent adventures required a group affair and some modern props that Krafft-Ebing had never heard of. She also had full knowledge that as to his own sex, Dee Dunstan's forays were much more frequent and much more suitable to his primary desires. So they got married and lived happily ever afterward.

I had become acquainted with Dee Dunstan through an introduction by his lawyer. Despite the protection of a wife, Dee Dunstan was frequently involved in nasty scrapes, and constantly had need of his lawyer's services. During one such scrape, his lawyer had brought me in, and I had been successful in quelling it with dispatch. Dee Dunstan had been highly appreciative, had thereafter regarded me as his own special agent, and had made it a practice to call on me even before he called upon his lawyer. Since he paid his fees promptly and well, I had no objection. I did my duty to the best of my ability, so much so, that I lost him as a client. I was instrumental, as it developed, in removing him from the jurisdiction. That was three years ago.

Three years ago, on a balmy Spring night, Dee Dunstan was moved to quit his house and essay forth in quest of surfeit for a pounding heart. By devious route, and after much roaming, he found himself, at two o'clock in the morning, in a comfort station of the Independent subway, but

Dee Dunstan found small comfort in the comfort station although he did find a peroxide-blond boy. Dee Dunstan had no sooner commenced preliminary dalliance behind the locked door of the coin-cubicle before there was an interruption in the shape of a huge gentleman from the Vice Squad. The huge gentleman reached in and collared them both. Perhaps he would not have collared quite so soon had he known who Dee Dunstan was, but collar he did, and he took them in.

I was awakened at three o'clock by an emergency call from Dee and I went downtown. Matthew Baxter, the District Attorney himself, was present. Matthew had been working late, and when Dee had identified himself, Baxter had been called in. Baxter had taken me aside and delivered himself as follows:

"Pete, I'm a practical man. I'm not looking for cheap publicity, I don't need it. There've been plenty of complaints about this Millay but most of the time we turned our heads the other way. First, it's tough to get a conviction on these things and second a guy like that doesn't actually do any harm, he only stinks up the joint. But I've had enough of it. This little fairy he picked up in the toilet happens to be a vagrant who's a hundred percent no good, but I've had enough. We'll prosecute even if we don't get a conviction. It'll hit the papers, there'll be a big stink, and Millay'll be marked lousy for life. It's not my nature to be cruel—I don't work that way—but I've had enough. This is the way it's going to be, and no other way. Either he gets out of town, once and for all, and for good—or we hold him and we prosecute. That's it, period. Now go talk to him."

I talked to him. I convinced him. Perhaps it had already been in back of his mind. Dee Dunstan Millay retired from show business, bought himself a vast estate in Havana, and became a country gentleman. He paid me a large fee for my puny efforts and considered me the hero who had delivered him from what he had thought was inescapable bondage. I did not disillusion him.

The plane bounced in for a smooth landing and I was in Havana. It was night and Havana is a lively town at night, especially in November, and night was no time to go calling on the Millays. I decided to get some sleep and call on the Millays in the morning. My hotel turned out to be hotel, night club, gambling casino, and house of joy. I did not get as much sleep as I had contemplated.

At eleven o'clock in the morning, breakfast for two was served in my room. I ate like a horse: it seems I had forgotten to eat the night before. Then I called Dee Dunstan

61

and his squeaks of pleasure over the phone were exhilarating. Great, great, great that I was in Havana and he'd send a car to pick me up at noon. I paid for everything—Mr. Duff was going to get a very queer statement of expenses—showered, shaved, dressed and checked out. At precisely noontime, the chauffeured car picked me up.

Dee Dunstan was in swimming trunks at the pool. He was chubby, with a dimpled face, a good-toothed smile, and a halo of brown hair around a shining bald pate. Mimi, in walk-shorts and a bandana, was seated at an umbrella table sipping what appeared to be a side-car.

"Hi!" She waved and returned to the side-car.

Dee ran up and kissed my cheek. "Great to see you, you old son of a bitch," he said. "Pale, you New Yorkers. Get your clothes off and lap up some sun. Got trunks?"

"No," I said.

"Over there," he said, pointing. "The cabanas. Find a pair that fit you. And don't worry, sweetie, they're all sterilized."

I swam in the pool and lay in the sun. Dee prattled about the delights of Havana and inquired hungrily about the delights of New York. Mimi joined us, a servant bringing her pitcher which was set in an ice keg, and glasses. "Drinkie?" Mimi said.

"What is it?" I said.

"Side-cars," she said. "Good morning drink. The lemon juice has vitamins. Citrus fruit is good for you."

We drank and we prattled and we swam and we lay in the sun and at two o'clock, dressed and refreshed, we had lunch in a cool spacious breeze-swept room. Mimi went up for a nap and only then Dee inquired, "What brings you, sweetie?"

"Katy Duff."

"Oh, she was our house-guest here for a month. Lovely kid. Only went back the other day."

"What's the story on that, Dee?"

"Pardon, sweetie?"

"What's with this house-guest routine? Did you know Miss Duff?"

"Never saw her before she came down here."

"So what's with this guest house routine?"

"Freddie sent her."

"For what?"

"She had a little trouble."

"Trouble? What kind of trouble?"

"She was slightly knocked up."

"What?"

"Slightly knocked up," he said.

There was brandy on the table and I nipped a bit. "Slightly knocked up," I said, "by whom?"

"I wouldn't know," Dee said.

"Freddie?"

"Honest, sweetie, I wouldn't know. I didn't ask. You see," he said, "down here it's different from the States. An abortion's no big deal, perfectly legal on the slightest kind of excuse. It's done in a hospital by a proper surgeon with proper nurses in attendance and proper care afterward. She stayed in the hospital for five days, which is more than plenty, and then recuperated here. She was running around like a calf a week later and when she left here she was as strong as a horse. A sweet kid."

"Who paid for it?" I said.

"I don't know," he said. "She brought her own loot."

"How far gone?"

"Four months."

That added a complication. Suzy had said that Katy had met Sylvester only a couple of months ago.

"I'm here," I said, "because her father sent me."

"Oh no," Dee said and looked frightened.

"Easy," I said. "It's just that she wasn't around for a month and she didn't tell him and he wants to know."

"Look," Dee said, "I told you. I'm not telling Papa or anyone else. You're a dear friend, sweetie. Papa? Let him go fry a fish."

"You don't have to tell Papa anything. But you don't mind if I earn a fee, do you, Dee?"

"Love you to earn a fee, sweetie."

"All I have to bring him is that she spent a month here as your house guest. No details, nothing else. That okay?"

"Sure. Of course."

"I'll need affidavits. From you and Mimi."

"Affidavits?"

"For the fee. Nothing special. Just that she was house guest here, and the dates. When she came and when she left. That's all. Am I asking too much?"

"Hell no, sweetie. As long as you don't want the addenda, I'll be most happy to co-operate. You want affidavits to the truth, you'll get affidavits to the truth. I love the truth. When do you want them?"

"Right now."

"What's the hurry?"

"I've got to go back to New York."

"Really, sweetie?"

"Really, really, really."

"Okay. Let's go wake up Mimi."

The chauffeur drove me to the airport, the plane was waiting, the trip was uneventful, and I took a cab directly

63

to the Waldorf, where I presented Edward Duff with the affidavits.

"Signed, sealed, notarized and certified," I said. "She couldn't have killed Sylvester. She was in Havana. Definitely."

"I told you," he said.

"Okay," I said, "and here's the expense account."

He looked at that. It was itemized. He looked back at me, smiled, went to a checkbook and wrote the check. He handed it to me and he said, "In due time, I'll go to the police about what I did. I hope, fervently, that I won't have to. I hope, fervently, that the thing will be cleared up. If it *is* cleared up, will you force me to go to the police anyway?"

"No," I said.

"Thanks," he said.

"Mr. Duff," I said, "you don't have to go back to the office, officially, until December One. You've had a couple of lousy days here. You look all shook up. Why don't you relax a little bit? Why don't you and I do the town somewhat?"

"Good idea," he said and straightened and smiled.

"How would you like to see *Flesh and Fury?*"

"I'd love it."

"Okay, that's for a starter. Stand by," I said and went to the phone and called Suzy. "I'm back," I said, "and I'd like to take Mr. Duff to *Flesh and Fury.*"

"You'll have house seats," she said. "They'll be at the box office."

"Grand," I said.

"And after the show, bring him to Royal House."

"Grand," I said.

"How are you?" she said.

"Sunburnt," I said, "in the craziest places. I'm open for inspection."

"I'll inspect you," she said. "See you later, lover."

"See?" I said to Duff. "Pays to know the right people. Who can get tickets to *Flesh and Fury* on a moment's notice?"

"Nobody," he said.

So that evening there was a fire backstage and the show closed down.

FOURTEEN

We HAD ARRANGED to meet, Duff and I, at eight-fifteen in front of the theatre. We met but we were part of a throng milling like the clothes-snatchers around the latest in sex-voiced crooners. The marquee lights were on but the theatre was closed. There was a large neatly printed sign declaring: CLOSED ON ACCOUNT OF FIRE. WILL RE-OPEN IN FIVE DAYS. TICKET ADJUSTMENTS MAY BE MADE AT THE BOX OFFICE AT ANY TIME WITH-IN SUCH PERIOD.

"Just goes to show you," Duff said. "It's the cycle I'm in."

"Yeah," I said. "Want to walk?"

"Love it," he said.

We crunched through dirty city snow. We walked to Fifth, breathing of the brisk air but not talking. We turned north on Fifth, still not talking. I wondered how much he knew about Havana, how much Katy had told him. He was not informing me. On the other hand, I was not informing him. If he knew, he knew. If he did not know, he was not going to know through me.

"I hear you called Suzy a few times," I said.

"Yes. As you said, I'm not due at the office until December first. I have time. I wanted to become acquainted with the young lady, kind of chat about Katy."

"She's the one that mailed Katy's letters for her."

"I know. Katy told me. I don't hold that against her. Quite the contrary. Any friend would do that for a friend."

"You're going to meet her, Daddy-o."

"Oh, good. When?"

"Practically now, I think. Probably meet a good many others of the cast of characters. Might put on more of a show for you than the show itself."

"Love it," Edward Duff said.

I flagged a cab and said, "Royal House."

Freddie Flanders was presiding at a long table in the rear. Champagne sprouted slender nozzles from silver icebuckets, but Freddie was working on Scotch and Freddie was already roaring drunk. Suzy was on his right, Linda on his left, and opposite were Nick Wallace and Tony Royal. I stole a glance toward Barker's table. Barker was there, with Janet Lewis.

"Well, the snooper," Freddie said. "Am I glad to see you. Who's your friend?"

"Edward Duff," I said.

"Duff? Duff?" Freddie said.

"Katy Duff's father."

"Well, now." Freddie rose and extended his hand. "I'm glad to know you, Mr. Duff." They shook hands. "Katy thinks you're God. Sit down, God. Join us. Glad to have you. The kid quit the show, didn't she?"

"Yes," Edward Duff said.

"Sit down, sit down. Drink up. Eat and be merry. We're having a party. We're celebrating a fire."

Duff sat near Nick Wallace. I snuggled near Suzy. She squeezed my thigh and smiled.

"What happened?" I said to Freddie. "What's with fire?"

"That restaurant next door, they got it in the kitchen, and the kitchen's contiguous with us backstage, so we got it too. The hell with it. The cast can use a five day vacation. Me too. Mr. Duff," he said, "meet everybody." He introduced each person at the table, including me. He gave the name, the occupation, and for each, he added a vicious line of comment. He saved Linda for last. "And this," he said, "is Linda Moreno, the star of our show. Linda is Nickie's girl friend, but Nickie's learned never to bat any eye, neither the right nor the left. You see, Linda's a cheater, and she cheats at the bat of an eye."

"You're drunkie, Freddie me boy," Suzy said.

"Leave him alone," Linda said. "If he weren't using the whiplash, it wouldn't be Freddie."

"Smartest thing you ever did, Mr. Duff," Freddie said.

"What?" Duff said.

"Getting your Katy out of this fetid atmosphere."

"Who makes it fetid?" Linda said.

"She hates me, this black-haired bitch. After all I've done for her—hates me."

"Me?" Linda said. "I love you Freddie."

"See that couple sitting over there." Freddie flicked a finger. "That's my partner Joel Barker and a gal in the show. Wanna know why they're not sitting here with us?" He pointed his thumb at Linda. "Because of her—Nick Wallace's gorgeous sweetheart."

"Cut it out," Nick said.

"Let him," Linda said. "Dear sick little Freddie, brilliant Freddie. If he doesn't get rid of his poisons, they'll consume him."

"She's a better dancer than you'll ever be."

"Keep it up," Linda said. "Someday I'll just naturally kill you."

"You wouldn't have the nerve. Plus you're too shrewd, too greedy."

"Don't strain yourself, Freddie," Linda said. "Drink up, you're losing your edge."

"See that kid over there, Mr. Duff? The one with Barker? She's Janet Lewis. She's good, real good. Barker brought her to me, and I auditioned her, and she was promised the lead in *Flesh and Fury*. Then this pimp here, this Tony Royal, introduces me to Mademoiselle Linda Moreno, and I flip my fool head, and now Linda's the lead, and Janet is an understudy. She hates me, this Janet, but it's hard to hate the boss—so she takes it out on Linda. Won't even sit at the same table with her."

"And Joel Barker?" Linda said. "He loves you?" She took a cigarette from a gold case, lit it, and blew smoke in Freddie's face.

"Hates me," Freddie said.

"He's paranoic," Linda said. "Everybody hates poor little Freddie."

"Hates me as much as Janet Lewis does, but it's an old hatred, and what can he do about it? I'm the brains, I'm the talent. He's a bookkeeper, and he's made a hell of a lot of dough out of it. He stinks too."

"Boy, you're really going tonight, Mr. Flanders," Tony Royal said.

Linda brought the cigarette to her red-wet glistening mouth, inhaled, and smoke trickled. "Something special is eating our Freddie," she said, "and he's covering up with even more than his usual nastiness."

"Mr. Duff," I said, "I told you this show would be better than the show we were going to see."

"There's snow in the mountains," Freddie said somberly and sat back and drained his glass.

"Snow in the mountains," Suzy said. "I know what you're thinking about. Why don't we? A real vacation."

"Yep," Freddie said somberly, "that's what I'm thinking about, a real vacation." He sat up, snapped his fingers at a waiter. "Come on, waiter, pour champagne for the people." Freddie poured Scotch for himself from a bottle on the table and added his own water. "We'll go up to the Lodge, all of us. We'll do skiing, and all the rest of that crap. We'll breathe clear, clean air, and we'll have fun, and we'll be revived. How's about it, everybody? A party up at the Lodge for a few days."

"I go only if my boy friend's invited," Suzy said.

"Of course he's invited, he's invited real special." Freddie turned to Duff. "Can you make it, sir?"

"Love it," Duff said.

"Great," Freddie said, growing animated. "Now here's how we'll work it. Tony, you'll supply the provisions."

"I'm invited too?" Tony said.

"You bet your ass," Freddie said. "Now here's how we work it, because it's impromptu. Tony, you'll supply the provisions from this restaurant of yours. Pack the stuff into that station wagon of yours, pick up Linda and Nick, and drive them up."

"When?" Tony said.

"Tonight, when you close. Your manager can take over for you for a few days, can't he?"

"Yes sir, he can."

"Fine. I'm paying. Don't worry, it's on me. Okay, that

takes care of the provisions, of Tony, Nick and Linda."

"How'll we get in?" Tony said.

"Barker'll be there before you," Freddie said.

Linda stood up. Most of the eyes of the patrons of Royal House turned toward her. Linda's dancer's figure was tightly wrapped within a beaded black dress, and it was like shimmering nakedness.

"Where you going?" Freddie said.

"To pack. That's your command, isn't it, Mon Herr? We're going for a vacation at four o'clock in the morning. Well, I've got to pack, haven't I? What I'm wearing is hardly fit for roughing it."

'Okay, you go with her, Nick. Tony, you'll pick them up at her apartment."

Linda and Nick said their au revoirs and went away.

"Tony," Freddie said, "you got a cook you can spare for us?"

"Yes, I have," Tony said. "A new man, a Chinaman. Terrific."

"Let's give him a smell of the mountain air too, huh?"

"You're the boss, Mr. Flanders. I'll go and attend right now."

Tony departed and that left Duff, Suzy, Freddie and me.

"Drink up, everybody," Freddie said. "I'll go straighten out Joel. There's a set of keys to the Lodge in the office. Joel will get them, he and Janet will pack fast, and they'll go off right away. Kind of prepare things for us. Pardon me."

That left Suzy, Duff and me. We watched as Freddie stiffly walked to Barker's table. Drunk or drunker, Freddie never staggered.

"Wow," I said.

"Genius at work," Suzy said. "What do you think, Mr. Duff?"

"I'm slightly overwhelmed," Duff said.

"He's a man of many facets, Mr. Duff," Suzy said. "There's another side to him—rather sweet and kind and charming."

"It's a side he's never displayed to me," I said.

"Maybe you rub him the wrong way," Suzy said.

"Why?" I said. "There's never been anything personal between us."

"You're my boy friend, remember?"

"So what?"

"It kind of pre-empts him. He's had eyes for me."

"Aah, you're the nutsiest," I said.

"Where is this Lodge?" Duff said.

"Not far," Suzy said. "In the Catskills. It's about a two and a half hour drive. It's lovely this time of the year."

And then Freddie was back.

"Okay," he said. "That department is taken care of. Now you folks, who'll drive?"

"Me," I said. "I'll take Mr. Duff and Suzy. We'll leave in the morning."

"Fine," Freddie said. "Now Suzy do me a favor."

"Yes sir, Mon Herr."

"Go over to my house and tell Ethel and Sara. Let them pack and pack for me. I'll drive them. In the morning."

"You sure you know what you're doing, Freddie?" Suzy said.

"Now come on, come on, get a move on," Freddie said. "Take the snooper. And leave Mr. Duff here. It'll be a pleasure to be talking to somebody who is not infected with the theatre."

Ethel was home as was Sara as was the ubiquitous Bruce Lawson. Suzy broke the news and Ethel was enthusiastic. "Wonderful idea," Ethel said. "I could do with a change, and I'm crazy for skiing. Who's coming?"

"Me," Suzy said, "my friend Chambers, Joel, Janet, Tony Royal and a cook, Nick Wallace, Katy Duff's father who is Mr. Edward Duff, you and Sara. Now start packing."

"When do we leave?" Sara said.

"Freddie's driving you. In the morning."

Ethel smiled toward Lawson. "Could you get away for a few days, Bruce?"

"Yes, as a matter of fact I can." Lawson's square-toothed boyish grin was bright. "But I won't be able to make it in the morning."

"Oh, Bruce," Sara said.

"I've got to be in Court," Bruce said. "On one of those insurance things."

"What time?" I said.

"I'm first witness, take the stand about ten. I should be on for about an hour. After that, I'm free."

"Look," Ethel said. "There's no difficulty. Freddie and I'll take off in the morning. Then, whenever you're finished in Court, Bruce, you can pick up Sara right here and drive up in the car. Sara knows the way. She'll be your pilot."

"Love it," Sara said. The kid was having a ball for herself. The lifeguard-type probably knew more maneuvers than the heavy spectacle type.

"Great," Bruce said and smiled again and squared his shoulders.

"Let's go, Suzy Q," I said. The guy was getting under my skin like a tick.

"Good bye, everybody," Suzy said, and I echoed her, and on the way to her apartment she said, "That guy affects you like a meat-grinder. What is it, professional jealousy?"

"Skip it," I said. "You left out Linda—in your resume to Ethel."

69

"On purpose," she said.

"What's the deal?"

"Freddie and Ethel."

"What about them?"

"Look, Freddie treats her like dirt. I know a lot about them."

"I thought you don't pry."

"I don't, but Sara talks to me a lot. About Freddie, the boss-man. He's a millionaire, but even with money he's the boss and an insulting boss. He gives Ethel whatever she wants, and Sara, but always, they've got to ask for it, always, some-how, they've got to demean themselves."

"So? She's married to him for a hell of a long time. She's used to it by now."

"But Freddie's never mixed oil and water before."

"Oil and water?"

"Look, there's been a lengthy procession of Lindas be-fore this Linda, but Freddie's always played it smart, he's never exposed Ethel to any of his numerous fair ladies. So . . . I didn't mention Linda."

"You think Ethel knows about her?"

"I wouldn't know, but I think that alcohol's finally bitten into his brain."

"Not Freddie. Of course he's excited."

"What makes you say that?"

"I think he killed a man. It kind of knocks you off bal-ance, unless it's your business."

"No. I think it's Nick Wallace, personally."

"What's Nick Wallace?" I said.

"He's a great beard, and I think Freddie feels protected with Nick squiring Linda. But I still think he's nuts."

"The nutsiest," I said. "Let's stop talking about Freddie. Let's talk about us."

"You love me?"

"I love you."

"You going to show me where you're sunburnt?"

"You bet."

"When?"

"Right now," I said.

FIFTEEN

WE DROVE AT a good clip, Suzy up front with me, Duff in the rear. The highway was clear, snow piled high on both sides—but the highway was clear and good for driving. The air had bite but the sky sat low, flat-grey and ominous. We kept climbing and we could feel the air grow more rarefied, and we lost the smell of the city, and there was a crisp winter fragrance about us.

"Looks like more snow," Duff said.

"Radio said a real blizzard's brewing," I said.

"Let it brew till we get there," Suzy said. "I'd hate crossing that bridge in a blizzard. I hate crossing that swinging monstrosity in the Summer with the sun shining. That thing terrifies me."

"What bridge?" Duff said.

"We're about twenty minutes away from it right now," I said. "Freddie's Lodge is near the town of Rexville, part of that municipality, as a matter of fact, but some distance away from it. About nineteen miles, they tell me. Fifteen miles from town, there's a thing called Gully's Gulch. That's a crack in the mountain, a narrow ravine that's practically got no bottom. They've got a bridge strung across it, one of those narrow wooden suspensions that swings with the breeze. Comes a storm, and down comes the bridge, and out come the townspeople to repair it. Never been an accident there yet, Suzy."

"Well, there will be someday," Suzy said.

"No. It's strong enough to carry weight. It's just that it gets unhinged when the big winds blow, but then, nobody uses it till it gets fixed up again."

"Once over the bridge, Mr. Duff," Suzy said, "then we're practically there. There's an old place called the Reynolds' House, and then there's nothing else, no other houses, just a four mile climb to Freddie's shack."

"Twenty-two rooms of shack," I said.

And then we were at the township of Rexville, and through the township of Rexville, and then we were at Gully's Gulch, and we rumbled over the slatty bridge, and we passed the locked up Reynolds' House, and we climbed the four miles to the Lodge, squat, spread, heavily built of rough oak. I blew the horn, and Joel Barker and Tony Royal, in winter duds but without coats, came out and helped us bring in our bags and stuff. "Everybody's here," Tony said. "Except Sara and her Bruce."

"Freddie made it this early?" I said.

"You know topsy-turvy Freddie," Tony said. "Who can figure Freddie?"

Red-headed Janet Lewis and serious Nick Wallace greeted us in the immense living room. "Hi, all," Janet Lewis said.

"Where's Freddie?" I said.

"In his den," Janet said. "That's where the whiskey is."

"And Linda?" I said.

"In her room," Nick said.

"Ethel?" Suzy said.

"In *her* room," Nick said.

"Let me tell you how I laid it out," Joel Barker rumbled. "We're all camped out on the first floor. One room for Ethel and Sara, Freddie's got his own room, Suzy and Pete have adjacent rooms—"

"Very cozy," Suzy said. "The hell with the way it's laid out. Show me where my room is, if you please. I'd like to clean up a little, huh?"

"Sorry," Barker said. "Come on. You too, Pete. Nick. Tony. Help with the stuff. Come along, Mr. Duff. You've got a real choice room."

"How do you know me?" Duff said.

Barker chuckled. "Freddie told me you were coming, and you're the only strange face."

"Glad to know you," Duff said.

"Likewise," Barker said. "Let's go, children."

It was good to be alone in the large lovely room: there was a smell of pine, a smell of oak, and the clean tingling smell of snow. I opened a window and breathed deeply and looked out at the snow-covered hills. Then I closed the window, opened my bag, took out a bottle of Scotch, and grabbed a slug from the bottle. I just did not want to get too healthy too quickly. Then I unpacked, hung my things away, filled the dresser drawers with the usual nonsense with which you fill dresser drawers, stripped down to shorts and underwear, washed up, and lay out on the bed. Somebody downstairs had set the boilers to going and the steam was coming up. I got off the bed, opened the window, took one deep breath of the health-giving mountain air, and lay on the bed again. I hoped, somehow, that Mr. Duff was comfortable.

Then there was a knock on the door.

"Come in," I called.

It was Suzy.

"Lie down," I said. "Make yourself comfortable."

"Oaf," she said.

"Uh huh," I said. "It's like that today. Excuse me." I got up off the bed and put on a bathrobe.

"I talked to Ethel," Suzy said. "She's furious."

"Forget it, will you. Let's have a vacation."

"And I talked to Linda. She's furious too. She didn't think that Ethel would be here. She figured if Freddie invited her, Linda—then it was because Ethel was engaged elsewhere."

"The hell with them all, for crying out loud. Kiss me, kid. We're in the country."

"Well, you can pour a drink for your guest." She looked meaningfully at the bottle set in the middle of the dresser like a doily. "Brought your own bottle, huh, you *shicker?*

72

Don't you have confidence in Freddie? There's enough liquor here to float a battleship, plus Tony brought up quite a stock."

"There are glasses in the toilet," I said with dignity.

She brought the glasses.

I poured.

Sara and Bruce arrived and everybody went skiing, except me. At least that's what I thought. I'm a city fella. To me, skiing is an outdoor manner of breaking your leg, and nothing else. But there were others who did not go skiing. Linda, Bruce, Freddie and I—we did not go skiing. I found out when I went down to the kitchen to eat. The Chinese cook prepared a wonderful Oriental dish entitled bacon and eggs and he concocted an exotic beverage called coffee. It was delicious and I told him so and while he was beaming at me, Linda strolled in wearing black lastex slacks and a clinging purple blouse, and brother, black lastex slacks and a tight purple blouse on Linda Moreno was enough to start spontaneous combustion in a castrated bull.

"Wow!" I said mildly amidst bacon and eggs.

Right behind her, like a puppy, trailed Bruce Lawson, and I'd swear his tail was wagging.

"You're the most beautiful woman I've ever seen," Bruce Lawson announced.

"And you're the most beautiful man *I've* ever seen," Linda countered in exquisite repartee.

"And I could live without *both* you beauties cluttering up my bacon and eggs," I said. "Why haven't you gone skiing?"

"Who needs skiing?" Linda said.

"I dig," I said and sipped coffee.

"I want to take pictures of her," Bruce Lawson said. "I brought all my equipment."

"For her, you'll need all your equipment, young fella," I said.

"No, seriously," Bruce said.

"In the nude?" I said innocently.

"Oh no," Bruce Lawson said just as innocently, the son of a bitch.

"He's a terrible lecher, this Chambers," Linda said hopefully. "Don't listen to him, Bruce."

"I'm not listening," Bruce said dutifully.

"Who else didn't go skiing?" I inquired.

"Only Freddie," Linda said.

"Where is he?" I said.

"In his study," Linda said.

"Okay," I said. "I'll tackle Freddie in his study, and you two tackle each other wherever you wish. But please get out of this kitchen. Let me eat."

73

Linda dunked my nose into the coffee, flounced once, but once was enough to set Brucie's eyes to popping like corn. She slithered out with My Own Brucie trailing behind like a spaniel afflicted with the heaves.

I finished my bacon and eggs, wiped up the plate with the toast, lit a cigarette to accompany more coffee, complimented the cook again, and went seeking Freddie. I found him: guess—in the study.

"Just the man I want to see," Freddie said, sipping from a darkly amber glass.

"First, please," I said. "I wish to admire this study. Every time I come here, I wish to admire this study."

"Admire," Freddie said.

It was a warm enormous room, all heavy oak, with free thick square beams running horizontally beneath the ceiling. Above the beams and along all four walls of the room was a narrow balcony, a spiral staircase in a corner leading up to it. The balcony was a sort of library, its shelves loaded with books. Freddie had them all, the greats and the near-greats: Hemingway, Faulkner, Camus, Spinoza, Goethe, Bertrand Russell, Eugene O'Neill, Aristophanes, Dostoevsky, Cervantes, Rider Haggard, Heywood Broun, Adam Smith, Dorothy Parker, Don Marquis, James Thurber, Sigmund Freud, Sterne, Swift, Marcus Aurelius, Melville, Hegel, Kant, Gibbon: he had them all, hundred upon hundreds of books. The library motif was further carried out beneath the balcony: one wall was entirely composed of crammed bookshelves. The wall opposite held a great wide brick fireplace with iron hooks protruding from its sides in a feudal design. The far wall was hung with hunting trophies and, on pegs, a good deal of Freddie's summer stuff: rope, rods, rifles and fishing equipment. The furniture was bulky and comfortable—Freddie's massive desk in the center of the room. The entrance door was large, perpendicularly oblong and thick: on either side was a bulging bar, filled to capacity.

"I've admired," I said.

"Sit down," he said. "Have a drink. I'm buying."

"Thanks a bunch," I said. "I appreciate."

He poured. I drank.

I poured. He drank.

Then he poured again and said, "Okay, what's the story?"

"What story?" I said innocently.

"Look, I'm quite disturbed about this."

"About what, Freddie?"

"You know about what, pal."

"You're going to have to say it, Freddie."

"Allan Sylvester," he said.

"Thank you, Freddie."

74

"Can you explain about Sylvester in the Bronx?"

"You mean in the Bronx instead of at Katy Duff's place?"

"That's what I mean."

"He was dead in Katy Duff's place."

"I know, I know."

"Thanks again, Freddie."

"Look, if you think you're being a snappy private sleuth drawing information out of me, you're an idiot. I know just what I'm saying to you, and I'm saying it because I want to. Now what's the bit with the Bronx, kid?"

I told him. I told him the entire story, complete and true, from beginning to end. "That's what brought Sylvester to the Bronx," I said.

"Got any more for me, kid?"

"You going to have anything for me, Freddie?"

"Maybe. Do you have any more?"

I told him about my trip to Havana. I said, "I brought affidavits to Duff, period. The affidavits stated that she had been the Millays' house-guest, and the dates. That cleared her of any possible involvement in the murder—at least as far as Mr. Duff is concerned. The affidavits stated nothing else, like her having been in a hospital."

"Does he know?"

"I didn't tell him."

"He's a man with guts," Freddie said. "I admire him."

"Me too," I said. "Anyway, he feels his daughter is in the clear. What the police may think may be very much different. The guy was dead in her apartment. She can be in Havana and yet, as an accomplice, be very much mixed up in it."

"I'll mix her out."

"Will you, Freddie?"

He poured. I drank.

I poured. He drank.

"Peter," he said, "I'm going to be something slightly foreign to me. I'm going to be noble."

"Why?" I said.

"Maybe because of this admirable Mr. Duff. Maybe because of Katy. Maybe because, in the end, it'll be no skin off my back. You say the cops played ball with you, told you about the twenty-two. Well, you're going to play ball right back at the cops. You're going to close their books on it, and it'll still be no skin off anybody's back."

"How're you going to turn that trick, Freddie?"

"I'm going to tell you what happened. And you're going to tell the cops. You're going to say that you cleverly drew it out of me while I was drunk. Most of it will check out, so they'll know you've got a true story. The killing part won't check out, because that part I'll deny, and since the

75

burden of proof is on them—they'll be stuck with the burden. The way I'll deny it, they'll know I did it—they just won't have an iota of proof; so, simply, they won't be able to hold me."

"Why would you want to do this, Freddie?"

He gazed into his drink like it was a crystal ball. "Because the way it was worked out, it stank. I had left a dead man in that kid's apartment, and I hated that. I didn't have the nerve to do anything about it. I just sat back and waited for the explosion. I knew she was in Havana, so that she really couldn't take the rap for it. But I'd stuck her in the middle, oh all unwillingly, and she was in for a heap of trouble. Then Sylvester turned up in the Bronx, and, of course, I was delighted all the way around the mulberry bush. Now you tell me that admirable old guy is going to go to the cops with it anyway. He did whatever he could to protect his kid, but he's got integrity. You, you louse, you've got integrity too. So, Freddie Flanders suddenly comes up with integrity—especially since no skin comes off the back. I say, among the three of us—the father, the eye, and the actual murderer—let's take the heat off that child."

"I understand, Freddie."

"You're welcome," Freddie said. "And let's get something else straight. I used the word murderer loosely. If I stood trial for what I did, no jury in the world would convict me. Homicide it was, but not murder, and justifiable homicide. But I won't stand trial because the hell with that. I don't have to. I'm human. We're all rather human, aren't we?"

"I understand, Freddie."

"You're welcome," Freddie said.

I poured for myself.

He poured for himself.

We both drank.

"This kid hit the show," Freddie said, "and she was slightly gorgeous, and I went on the make. Pushover, of course. A kid. But a sweet kid. We had a little fun, and then I was through. But the kid was a kid and didn't know how to take care of herself. She didn't tell me, not for a long while, because the romance was no longer a romance."

"She met Sylvester a couple of months ago, didn't she?"

"Yes. There was no question that her problem was . . . er . . . my problem."

"I didn't mean that," I said. "What I'm wondering about is—did she tell him about her . . . er . . . problem?"

"I'll come to that."

"Fine. Excuse the interruption."

"Okay. She had a problem. It was my problem. So I saw her through it. I called Dee Dunstan and had him make arrangements for her. That can be verified. I gave

76

her a check for four thousand dollars which, as a matter of fact, she cashed in my bank with my okay. That can be verified—the cancelled voucher is in my files. The entire Havana thing can be verified—and my connection with it."

"What can be verified about your connection with the death of Allan Sylvester?"

He smiled wryly. "Only that I owned a twenty-two which I don't own any more. Only that I . . . er . . . lost that twenty-two. That, coupled with the story that you so devilishly drew out of me while I was swacked—which of course I shall deny. I shall, of course, be forced to admit the Havana part of the story—so, if they reason correctly, since that part is true, and you drew that part out of me—certainly they'll believe that you drew the rest out of me, although that I deny, and that they won't be able to prove."

"You're taking a chance, Freddie."

"I don't believe so, pal. I tell you they can't prove a thing. It's impossible."

"What happened, Freddie?"

"This Sylvester was a real cool one, and death on dames. The kid was on the bounce from me, and this guy was a real big-time charmer. Anyway, as it turned out, she had told him about her problem. Of course, he played it cool, lay low, and stayed in the background. She went to Havana, was there practically a month, and then he called me."

"When?" I said.

"This past Tuesday. The minute he mentioned his name, I knew it was trouble. He said he wanted to see me. I asked him where. He said at her apartment. Right then—and I didn't have to be intuitive—I knew what it was all about."

"And you went?"

"Sure I went. First I called down to Havana. She was still there. So I knew he was working alone. The appointment was for five-thirty. I went, but I packed my trusty old little old twenty-two, pardner."

"Any idea you were going to use it?"

"I had no idea about anything except that I was burning mad. Anyway, he opened the door for me, sat himself down on the couch, took out that big automatic and pointed it at me so that I'd give him rapt attention. Captive audience, as it were."

"So you got slightly madder, I take it."

"Slightly. Then he made with the pitch. He told me the kid was seventeen and a half, under age. I admit I knew that—but I didn't know it at the beginning. She'd registered with the show as nineteen—and she looked every bit of it."

"I know. I've seen her."

"Very carefully, he expounded to me that it was statutory rape, and that my sending her for the thing in Havana

77

only compounded the felony. Before he even began to make his requests for the old dinero, I asked whether Katy knew what he was doing. He said no, that he wasn't looking to share any of the proceeds with her. Once we made a deal, he said, he'd even see to it that she went home, and got out of both our lives. On the other hand, if I didn't make a deal, he'd get the right people to do the talking, people like columnists and newspaper guys, and once the D.A. took her in for questioning, the kid would of course crack wide open. It wouldn't be any fun for me, he explained."

"It wouldn't be," I said.

"Damn right it wouldn't be," Freddie said.

"And he had it worked out real clean and neat without any involvement on his part."

"Oh, he had me by the well-known nuts, no question."

"How much did he want?"

"A hundred thousand dollars."

"Wow." I whistled.

"Pete, if he'd have asked for five, ten thousand bucks, I think I'd have played along. A thing like that, busting wide open in the papers, couldn't do me a bit of good. I've paid for my pleasures, paid through the nose, plenty of times in my life. But his colossal nerve in demanding a figure like that, his cool easy manner, his certainty that he had me flat on my ass—I think that triggered it. I'm not a fighter—I believe in compromise—but I got just mad enough to want to fight. Pretty stupid, eh?"

"Oh, I don't know."

"I could have gotten killed."

"But he did, didn't he? What'd you do?"

"I played it just as cool as he. I've been in the theatre most of my adult life. I'm probably as good an actor as most of my actors. I played it perfectly. I told him that he had me, that he was a son of a bitch, but that he had me, that circumstances, somehow, had worked out perfectly for him. I said that he wasn't clever, that he was in the right spot at the right time—and that he had me. Then I asked him for assurances, in case I paid."

"Smart enough," I said.

"He said he knew the law. Once she got out of town, grew a little older, got past eighteen, and hadn't made complaint —in those circumstances the law couldn't give me any trouble. He said he'd be willing to take twenty thousand down and twenty thousand the first of each month thereafter. After I'd made the first payment, I could check with the lawyers and I'd see he was right. Furthermore, he said, once I'd made that first payment, I'd have an investment to protect, and I'd keep paying. Quite the son of a bitch, eh?"

78

"Quite," I said.

"Figured me for a real easy sucker."

"Yep," I said. "So?"

"I told him he had a deal, asked if he'd take a check. Sure, he said, the acceptance of a check is no mark of a crime. Sure, he said, you got a checkbook with you? Sure, I said, I have, I was expecting something like this. He snickered and waited, all easy and sure of himself. I reached in for my checkbook but I didn't whip out my checkbook, I whipped out my trusty twenty-two. I shot him before he knew he was being shot. I was lucky. The slug hit him where it counted. He just sat there, dead."

"And you?"

"I got out of there."

"Fingerprints?"

"Oh, I wiped things up, don't worry. Slammed the door and it was locked on the clicker, period."

"Then?"

"Took me a ride on the Staten Island ferry. Dismantled the twenty-two and dropped it into the river, piece by individual piece. Nobody in the world can hang that gun together, and nobody in the world can hang this thing on me."

"Freddie," I said, "sometimes you're a great man."

"Why, because I killed a cockroach?"

"No. Because you've told me. And because of your motives in telling me."

He grinned, almost sardonically. "That kid didn't have it too good in New York. First me, and then that Sylvester. A scandal on top of it—too much, too much. Can you imagine, Pete, my bewilderment when I read that they'd found him in the Bronx?" And then, suddenly, he was the cold-eyed, flush-faced, brusk Freddie I knew. "Okay," he said. "Now do me a favor and get the hell out of here. You know what you're supposed to do when you get back to town. Do it. Now get the hell out of here."

"They'll call you in, Freddie. They'll give you trouble."

"That'll be my trouble," he said. "I've a hunch I'll enjoy it."

SIXTEEN

THE SKIERS RETURNED late, rosy-cheeked and sparkling-eyed, but it was no use. This was one party that was foredoomed to failure. Little Sara sulked because she had lost big Brucie. Ethel stole about trying to keep out of Linda's way. Linda stole about trying to keep out of Ethel's way. Brucie trudged after Linda as if she were wearing catnip and he was a pussy. Freddie noticed the burgeoning romance and blamed Nickie. Nickie, trying to keep out of Freddie's way, made a play for Suzy. Suzy, perhaps because she was sorry for Nickie, patted him and leaned her body close. That brought me up short and surly. Tony Royal, trying to get between Linda and Bruce, grew attentive to Linda, and that had Freddie storming again, railing against both Tony *and* Nickie. Janet Lewis, with her penchant for older men, clung to the stranger in our midst—Edward Duff. That had Joel Barker spitting out fingernails.

And through it all, Freddie kept drinking.

Freddie was sodden, but Freddie kept drinking.

Everybody was drinking, and occasionally eating.

The Chinese cook was the busiest man in the house.

The snow began. The radio said the blizzard was on its way.

Suddenly, a fist fight erupted between Nickie and Freddie. Ethel intervened. She was taller than either of them, and probably stronger.

"You're fired," Freddie said to Nickie. "Get out of this house."

"Oh, now stop it," Joel said.

"I want this punk out of here."

"Look, you're not telling him to leave your house on Sixty-second Street. We're up in the mountains with a blizzard coming on, and he doesn't even have a car, as a matter of fact. You know as well as I do he came up in Tony's station wagon."

"All right. Let him stay. But let him keep out of my way. And he's fired. As of now." And with that Freddie stalked off to his study and he didn't come out of his study. People went in to see him, but he did not come out. Not once.

And then the blizzard started. It howled.

It was something to see through the storm windows.

"I'm going to bed," Ethel said. "Coming Sara?"

"Yes, Mother," Sara said.

It was only eight o'clock in the evening, but we were all dog-tired.

Then Tony opened a window to see how things were doing. Blinding snow churned. Wind screeched.

"Shut that window," Joel Barker ordered.

Tony shut the window. "I'm going to sleep," he said.

"We're all going to sleep," I said. "What about Freddie?"

"In the study," Linda said, "getting drunker and drunker."

"How do you know?" Barker said.

"I was just there," Linda said.

Duff stretched, said, "Good night, all. See you in the morning."

Five minutes later, I went up after him. I knocked and he called, "Come in."

I went in. "Got news," I said.

"Sit down, Mr. Chambers."

I sat and I told him. I told him the whole damned bit. All the way. Complete. He did not move a muscle. Maybe he felt secure about Katy. She was in California by now. She was probably on her way to Honolulu or to wherever else he had sent her. Distance lends enchantment. Edward Duff looked enchanted.

"We've got a great story for the police now," I said. "It'll cover up your obstructing justice. They can close their book after what I tell them."

"Strange man," he said.

"Who?" I said.

"Flanders."

"Mr. Duff," I said, "did you know about . . . Havana?"

"Havana?" he said.

"Katy's problem?"

"Yes," he said.

"She told you?"

"She told me everything. All of it. She also told me that she had learned about Sylvester, what a heel he was. The poor kid. Her adventure in New York turned out to be a frightful nightmare. That's why she was ready to run, flee, go to school, be a nice little girl. She was a kid yearning for life, and life caught up with her—far too early. Poor Katy."

"Yeah," I said. "She told you about . . . about Freddie?"

"First Freddie, then Allan Sylvester. Nice indoctrination." He was silent. I was silent. "You know something," he said. "Funny. This was a wild little girl, but she was a virgin until she met Freddie Flanders." He tightened his mouth. A spasm in his jaw lumped a muscle.

Outside the wind howled.

"Good night, Mr. Duff," I said and I stood up. "Get a good night's sleep."

"Thank you for everything," he said.

I went to my room and I got out of my clothes and I showered. I lay out on the bed and picked up one of the books I had brought. It was William James' *The Principles of Psychology*. "Really?" I said to myself. "When was I moved to buy this one?" But I read, doggedly. I was up to *The Functions of the Brain* when I answered to an impulse. Perhaps it was the influence of James. I closed the book and looked at the clock. It was only nine-fifteen. I got out of the bed, opened my door, and looked out. The house was dark. The entire first floor was dark. I went to the stairs and looked down. Dark, except for the thin slice of light coming from beneath the door of Freddie's study. Everybody's asleep, I thought, except Freddie. And for a moment, I thought: poor Freddie.

I went back to my room and decided to go to sleep. I

flicked off the light switch, and instantly there was a knock on my door. I flicked the switch back on and opened the door. It was Suzy. She was dressed in nothing.

"Look at you," I said.

"What's with me?" she said.

"You're naked," I said.

"What do you think you are?" she said.

"I'm in my own room," I said.

"This is the way I sleep," she said. "You ought to know."

"You're not sleeping now," I said.

"I couldn't sleep," she said. "I'm scared. That wind outside, this house, the people, I'm scared to death. God, I'm glad you're here."

"I love you," I said.

"I love you," she said.

I switched off the light.

We lay together like children.

We did not make love. We lay together like frightened children. The room was warm. The wind howled faintly outside. Inside, the hiss of the steam seemed louder. Perhaps we slept. I think we slept.

But then the screams came.

Scream after pealing scream.

Scream after horrible scream.

SEVENTEEN

I GRABBED AT a robe, snapped on the lights. It was exactly midnight. Suzy struggled into a pair of my slacks, knotted them about her middle, and covered her top with a turtleneck sweater.

Then we ran.

Lights blazed, doors slammed, there was the pounding of running feet.

Downstairs, wrapped within a thick bathrobe, Sara was standing in front of the open door of Freddie's study, screaming. Her hands were at her face, her nails dug into the skin of her cheeks: she stood rigid, screaming. Then she collapsed.

The first to get to her were Joel Barker and Ethel. Ethel snatched a glance into the room, sobbed retchingly, bent to Sara. Joel took a look, said, "Stay out of here," and went in. I went in after him. Then Tony, Nick, Bruce and Duff were there. "Keep the women out," Joel barked. Nick went to the threshold, waved Linda and Janet away, pushed Suzy out, closed the door and leaned against it.

"My God," he said, looking upward.

Freddie Flanders was hanging by his neck from one of the beams, his face blue, his eyes protruded, his veins distended, his lips drawn back from his clenched teeth in a grinning grimace of death. Rope, which had hung on a peg on the far wall, was now around his neck, deeply imbedded, and a kicked-away chair was beneath him. The rope had been flung over one of the great square beams, and the other end of the rope, taut as a stretched wire, was securely knotted to one of the hooks that were part of the design of the fireplace. There he dangled, Freddie Flanders, like a puppet on a string: small, slender, stiff and lifeless, the wrenched grin giving a sardonic expression to his face even in death.

"My God," Nick Wallace repeated, and his breathing was noisy.

Bruce Lawson righted the chair, stood on it, and gingerly examined Freddie. "He's dead," he said.

"Don't touch him!" Joel said.

Bruce came down off the chair.

"What do we do?" Tony said. "Do we cut him down?"

"You leave him alone," Barker said. "Pete!"

"Yes, sir?"

Joel Barker had finally come into his own. That dangling figure—dead—had finally released Joel Barker into his own. Joel Barker was the Chief, The Commander, The Authority. There was no one in that room who did not realize that Joel Barker was in charge.

"Pete," he said quietly, "call the police. As for the rest of you, I think you'd better all clear out of here."

I went to the phone.

Bruce Lawson said, "Just a minute, Mr. Barker—"

I said, at the telephone, "Phone's dead, Joel."

"Yes," Barker said, "the wires are probably down. I've been here before during storms like this. Mr. Duff."

"Yes, Mr. Barker?" Duff said.

"There's a phone in every room in the house. Try them all, if you please. If one's dead, they're probably all dead. But try them anyway, would you please?"

"Yes, sir. Of course." Duff went out and closed the door behind him.

"You were saying, Mr. Lawson?" Barker said.

"I've got a camera, flash-bulbs and film upstairs in my suitcase," Lawson said. "This sort of thing, well, somehow, it's my business, as it is Mr. Chambers'. I didn't know the phones were out of commission but I did realize, in this weather, it would take the police quite some time to get here—nineteen miles or more in this impossible weather. Now that the wires are down, I think it's even more important."

"Get to the point, please," Barker said.

"I think that the quicker pictures are taken, the better it would be. The police would appreciate it."

Barker turned to me. "What do you think?"

"He's a hundred percent right," I said.

"I'll do exactly what the police would do if they were here. I'll get shots of this thing, close and far, and from every angle," Bruce said.

"All right, get your stuff," Barker said.

"We're going to go after the cops by car," I said. "It's going to take time, going and coming. The best photos are those taken closest to . . . to the time of the event."

"Okay!" Barker said to Lawson. "Get your stuff!"

"Is there a ladder in the house?" Lawson said. "I'll need a ladder."

"Tony," Barker said. "There's a ladder in the basement. Get it up here."

Tony and Lawson went out, and Duff came in.

"All dead," Duff said.

"Where are the women?" Barker said.

"In the kitchen, except Miss Moreno. She's in the living room, alone. Miss Flanders . . . somewhat in a state of shock, I think."

"Poor kid," Barker said.

"Look," Nick Wallace said, pointing up at Freddie.

"What?" Barker said.

"What's that white thing sticking out of his pocket?"

A corner of white paper protruded from a side pocket of Freddie's jacket.

Laboriously, Barker climbed onto the chair beneath Freddie.

"Hey," I said.

"What?" Barker said.

"You're not supposed to touch," I said.

"I'll take the responsibility," Barker said. "You're all witnesses to what I'm doing."

He reached up and pulled the paper from Freddie's pocket. "It's from his memo pad," he said. "Here, give me a hand."

I helped him down.

"Your prints are going to be on it," I said.

"Okay, so my prints are going to be on it. You're all here, aren't you? You all know *how* my prints came on it?"

"Do we?" I said.

Bruce came with his equipment.

Tony came with the ladder.

"He killed himself, all right," Barker said.

Thinly Duff said, "Well, you didn't think he was *murdered* like that, did you?"

"Poor Freddie," Barker said. "This is in his handwriting. Listen." He read: " 'A suicide is a person who has considered his own case and decided that he is worthless and who acts as his own judge, jury and executioner and he probably knows better than any one else whether there is justice in the verdict.' Poor, tormented, little Freddie."

"I suggest you put that note in the desk drawer," I said. "And nobody else touches it."

"Good idea," Barker said. He put the note into a drawer of Freddie's desk. "All right, Mr. Lawson, go to work. Then we'll all get out of this room."

Tony opened the ladder and Lawson went to work. He took full shots, angle shots, close shots. He climbed the ladder and took tight shots of Freddie, of the rope, of the beam. He descended and took pictures of the room, of Freddie from various angles of the room, re-ascended and took many close-ups again. He used up all the film, five rolls.

"Finished," he said.

"Fine," Barker said. "Tony! Get this ladder out of here. Mr. Lawson, get your stuff out of here, and please remember you're responsible for the photographs." He looked from one to the other of us, individually. "We're all leaving this room now, and none of us comes back. We'll leave everything as is until the police arrive. None of us has any further business in here. Is that agreed?"

"Agreed," we chorused.

He led us out and closed the door behind him.

EIGHTEEN

SARA SAID HALTINGLY: "I have taken a sleeping pill. I had fallen asleep almost at once. I slept but through it all I was having terrible nightmares. I awoke, suddenly, with a start. I put on the bed lamp. Mother was asleep in the other bed. I tried to sleep. I couldn't. I decided to go down for a glass of warm milk. I looked at the clock. It was almost midnight. I put on my robe and went down. I put on some lights, in the living room and in the kitchen. I saw the light coming from under the door of Freddie's study. 'Poor Freddie,' I thought, 'still up, still probably drinking, while all of us are snug in our beds.' I thought I'd ask him if he wanted some milk and perhaps a sandwich. I knocked. There was no answer. I opened the door . . ."

She sobbed, pressed her hands to her face.

Barker said, "You'd better take her upstairs, Ethel. And, if I may, I suggest you remain there with her until the police come."

"Yes, of course," Ethel said.

"The phones are out of order," Barker said, "because of the storm. Some of the men shall have to drive into Rexville for the police."

"I see," Ethel said. "I'll be in my room with Sara."

Janet helped hold Sara, and they practically carried her upstairs. Janet returned very quickly, said to Barker: "Anything I can do?"

"Nothing. I think we should confine ourselves to our rooms as much as we can, until the police business is over."

"Very well," Janet said and went back upstairs.

In the living room, Linda Moreno was getting drunk on huge gulps of brandy from a water tumbler. She was very pale.

"Upstairs," Barker told her. "Whoever isn't doing something, should be out of the way. You too Suzy. Please."

Linda re-filled the glass and left the room.

Suzy said, "You sure there isn't anything I can do?"

"Nothing," Barker said.

"Good night, then."

So now it was a council of war: six men in the living room.

"Got the photos and stuff out of the way?" Barker asked Lawson.

"Yes, sir," Lawson said. "In my room."

"All right then," Barker said. "Who goes for the police?"

"Me," Lawson said.

"Me," Tony said.

"Me," Nick said.

"I've got a suggestion," I said.

"Yes, Pete?" Barker said.

"It's murder out there," I said. "There can be a lot of trouble, driving. I suggest we go in force. Bruce, Tony, Nick and myself. That'll leave you and Mr. Duff here to take care of the fort."

"Fine," Barker said. "And don't forget, each of you, to take flashlights. Okay, now go up and get dressed, and dress warmly."

"We'll use my car," Bruce said. "When Sara and I got to Rexville this afternoon, I had the garageman there stick my chains on, just in case."

"Swell," Barker said. "Now get a move on, fellas."

Ten minutes later, while we waited in the foyer, Bruce went out for the car. "Be with you in a minute," he said. "Car's around the back." He was huge in a mackinaw, ski pants and a ski cap.

He returned almost at once.

"Car here already?" Nick said.

"Sure, come on."

"Didn't hear a thing," Tony said. "Didn't hear you start the car, didn't hear the clink of chains, didn't even hear you pull up in front."

"Heavy snow like that," Bruce said, "it's insulation, pads the sound. Plus the wind. Come on, huh?"

Barker called: "Good luck!"

86

The trip was bad, but I had expected worse. The headlights gave off a sort of swirling visibility, but we could see. Our progress was slow, but we made it to the bridge without untoward event. I peered through the windshield and I said, "I'm afraid that damned bridge is down."

Bruce moved the car almost to the brink of Gully's Gulch and braked. "Let's get out for a look," he said.

The four of us got out, flashlights in hand, leaving the doors of the car hanging open. The wind blew and the bridge swung like a hammock, deeply sagging, loose at the far end.

"Ain't really down," Tony said. "Just drifting."

"Loose on the other side," Nick said.

"Loose, drifting, sagging, swinging—we can't get across," I said.

"That's a cinch," Tony said.

"What now?" Bruce said.

"They fix these things pretty much in a hurry," Nick said. "I've heard Freddie talk about this damn bridge."

"So what do we do?" Tony said.

"We go back," I said, "and keep trying the phone. They'll have the wires up before this bridge gets strung straight, that's for sure."

Wind whipped, the car door slammed, and Nick screamed. "My finger's caught! Jeez-us! Get that door open!"

I pulled hard, against the wind. The door opened enough for Nick to get his finger out. He jumped up and down, bent double, one hand clasped about the other. The gleam of Bruce's flash showed blood running down the fingers. "What's that house?" Bruce said. "Over there. Tony, do you know?"

"Some broken-down millionaire's shack. Empty. They ain't used it in years."

"Let's get him over there, fast."

Bruce sprinted ahead. Tony and I took Nick under each arm and dragged. "The Reynolds' House they call this joint," Tony mumbled. Bruce used his flashlight to break a pane of glass out of a window, inserted his hand, turned the catch, lifted the window and climbed in. We heard him at the locks of the door, and then it opened.

I lay Nick on the floor, groaning in pain. We turned our flashlights on the finger: it was the index finger, badly smashed and bleeding profusely. I gave my flash to Bruce. Tony sat on the floor and held Nick's head. I ripped a handkerchief into strips and knotted it over his wrist. I pulled as tightly as I could and held on. Nick groaned. Tony said, "Easy, kid." After a while, the hand blanched and the

87

bleeding stopped. I used Tony's handkerchief as a bandage. Then we got Nick to his feet.

"What a night," Tony said.

"I don't feel it any more," Nick said. "Is it bad?"

"I seen worse," Tony said. "Let's get the hell out of here."

Barker and Duff were dressed when we got back, and there was hot coffee in the kitchen. We told them what had happened, and what had happened to Nick. Duff took over with Nick, cleansed the finger, applied antiseptic and bandaged it gently. Nick winced in pain.

"I feel it again. Man, do I feel it!" he said. "Is it bad, Mr. Duff?"

"It'll keep till morning, Mr. Wallace, until we can get some professional help. It's not good, I'll say that. That bone may be broken and there's a lot of flesh mashed up."

"How about some coffee?" Bruce said.

"Yes," Nick said.

We had coffee all around.

Then Tony said, "Nickie, why don't you go to bed?"

"Yeah," Nick said.

Barker smiled. "In case it'll help with your recovery, you're re-hired as press agent, and I promise you you'll never be fired again as summarily."

"Thanks," Nick said.

"Come on, Nickie," Tony said. "I'll dose you with two, three aspirins and help you get into the hay. You're an invalid now."

"Thanks," Nick said.

We had more coffee.

Bruce looked toward the window. "Stopped snowing," he said. He opened the window. "And it's kind of stopped blowing," he said. "I think our blizzard's over."

"Short and sweet," Duff said. "Don't get much of this in my neck of the woods."

"Where you from?" Barker said.

"California," Duff said.

Tony returned with a report. "Nick's laid out nice and comfy. I looked in on the others. Sara and Mrs. Flanders are up and that Sara's in pretty bad shape, still half-hysterical. Janet's sleeping. Linda's sleeping and smelling of booze. Suzy's in bed, reading. What do we do now, Mr. Barker?"

"We go to our rooms and try to get some sleep, except one of us."

"Which one?" Tony said.

"The one that's elected to keep trying the telephone."

"I'll take that job," I said. "I'm a night-bird type anyway.

I'll hit that phone every fifteen minutes until I get through."

"Fine, thanks, Pete," Barker said. "If you get tired, wake me and I'll take over for you."

In a hushed voice, Tony said: "What about . . . Freddie?"

"Nobody goes into that studio until the police come," Barker said.

"Geez, what a bit?" Tony shuddered, massaging palm against palm. "Freddie Flanders, hanging like a pigeon caught on a telegraph wire. Freddie Flanders, the dangling man, just hanging there. Geez, I bet he'd hate it if he knew it. It's . . . it's undignified."

"Let's go," I said.

Barker turned off the lights.

It was two-thirty in the morning.

NINETEEN

IN MY ROOM, I picked up the phone. It was dead. The snow was coming down again, and the wind was raging. We had been premature. The blizzard had abated but it had not ceased. I paced about like a schoolboy cramming for an exam. I tried to collect the facts in my head and sort them out. Things had happened so fast, there had been no time to think. I tried to think. I was in no shape for it. It was like the schoolboy trying to cram facts into a tired brain. I gave up studying for my test.

I went out into the corridor and knocked on Suzy's door. Suzy opened, said, "Hi."

"I'm on telephone duty," I said. "I'm elected to hit the horn every fifteen minutes until somebody answers. Want to sit out the vigil with me?"

"If that's what you call it," she said.

"That's what I call it," I said.

"Boy, you're grumpy, aren't you?"

"Yeah, grumpy," I said. "Coming?"

"Sure, but hold up a minute," she said. "After all, I owe you a turtle-neck sweater and a pair of pants."

At five-thirty, the snow stopped, the wind ended, the sky grew clear. At six o'clock, the phone was alive. I asked the operator for the police at Rexville and was quickly connected. A young man's voice sleepily said, "Police. Rexville."

"I want to report a suicide," I said.

"Huh? What's that?"

"Suicide," I said.

"Suicide?" Sleep went out of the voice. "Where? Who's this?"

"My name is Peter Chambers. I am a guest at the Flanders' house."

"Over Gully's Gulch? Flanders?"

"That's right," I said.

"Who's the suicide?"

"Mr. Flanders."

"Flanders hisself! Hey, hang on a minute, I'll let you talk to the Chief."

"Chief?" I said. "How efficient can a police force get? The Chief is up this early?"

"Not usually, but there's a crew out working on the bridge. It's an emergency, if you know what I mean, sir. When it's an emergency, the Chief is up. Hang on, please."

Then a new voice came on, clipped as a crew-cut. "Yes? What is it?"

"Who's this?" I said, mostly for spite.

"Chief of Police. The name is Adam Cole. Now what is it, please?" I told him.

"Okay," he said. "We've got men working on the bridge. Ought to be in shape in a couple of hours. We'll be out there first thing. You keep things exactly as they are."

"They've been that way all night, Chief. We discovered him at midnight."

"Good, good. Okay, man, you're tying up my wire."

"May I tie up your wire for another little instant, dear Chief?"

"What? What's that?"

"We've got an injured man here. Will you bring out a doctor too?"

"Sure will, fella, Coroner. Coroner's a doctor too. Flanders you said, didn't you?"

"That's what I said."

"Figure it for two hours. Thank you. Good bye."

He hung up.

I said to Suzy, "You'd better get out of here. People will talk."

"Look at him," she said. "Real proud because I bust my way in here."

"That's no language for you, sweetheart. It's too easy to make jokes when you use language like that. Scram. I'm going to wake Joel. And thanks for the return of the pants."

"It was nothing."

I kissed her and put her out. I washed up and went to Barker's room. I kept knocking until he answered, pouch-faced from sleep.

"Phone's in shape," I said. "I got through. They're working on the bridge. Police should be here in a couple of hours. Chief's name is Adam Cole. Must have a strong personality. I'm talking like him."

"You get any sleep?" Barker said.

"Nope."

"Want to grab a little now?"

"Nope. I've been chewing Dexedrine. I'm wide awake."

"Two hours you said?" He looked at his watch. "Okay, Pete. Thanks for the night's work. I'll take over now. I'll wake them at seven."

At seven it got as busy as a prophylactic station after shore leave. There was the tramping of feet, the sounds of running showers, doors opening and closing, the calls for the borrowing of after-shave lotion, the calls for the borrowing of lipstick, the clatter of dishes in the kitchen, the sounds of "Good morning," and over all, the delightful smells of sizzling bacon, frying sausages, heating hotcakes, and perking coffee. Suzy came down looking like a doll. Janet came down looking like a doll. Bruce Lawson came down looking like a doll.

"Breakfast in bed for Miss Moreno," he said. "I'm to bring it. Juice, bacon and eggs, toast, coffee."

"Coming up," said the Chinese cook.

"You going to spoon-feed her, Handsome?" Tony said.

"Look out you don't get your finger bit," Nick said. The bandage had been soaked through with blood. Duff had arranged a sling and Nick was wearing the hand within the sling.

I heard Barker say softly to Ethel, "I haven't had a chance to tell you how sorry I am about all this, sorry for you."

"I know, Joel," she answered.

"How's the kid?" Barker said.

"Not good at all," Ethel said. "She needs a doctor."

"There's a doctor coming," Barker said.

Barker was in charge. He rode herd on everybody. At eight o'clock of a fine bright winter morning we were all sitting in the living room—clean, washed and fed—waiting.

And at ten after eight, the police arrived.

Adam Cole was tall, lean and angular with the bright eyes of a terrier. There were four other men with him. One of them carried a little black bag.

"I'm Chief Cole," he announced.

"Yes, sir," Barker said. "This way, please. He's in the study."

"Just a minute," Cole said. "Who're you?"

"I'm Joel Barker. Mr. Flanders' business partner."

"Good enough. You know that Rexville's the county seat here, and this house is within the area. We have complete and exclusive jurisdiction. Is that understood?"

"Yes, sir."

"This gentleman is Dr. Frank York, who is our coroner.

The other three gentlemen are my deputies. One of them's the town undertaker. He's got his hearse outside. We're going to have to take the body in for autopsy. You'll notice I'm a man who likes to make things clear and come to the point quickly. Any questions?"

"No, sir," Barker said. "This way, please."

"Not yet," Cole said. "These all the people that was in the house?"

"Yes, sir."

"Nobody else?"

"Nobody else."

"Now I want the name, address and occupation of every person here. Quickly now. You can each talk for yourselves." He listened intently, as one of his deputies made notes, his intelligent mobile face registering his reactions. He had most respect for the banker, Edward Duff. He had diminishing respect for the people of the theatre. And he had no respect at all for the insurance investigator and the private detective. "Okay," he said, "thanks. Now where is he?"

"In his study," Barker said. "Right across the foyer. This way, please."

Barker led them to the door and opened it.

Freddie Flanders lay face down on the floor.

There was no rope around his neck.

There was no rope anywhere to be seen.

TWENTY

WORDS FLEW LIKE buckshot. Words cascaded in confusion. Barker, Nick, Bruce, Tony—words overlapped words—and over all Adam Cole was roaring: "Quiet! Quiet, everybody! Quiet!" And suddenly there was stillness, utter stillness.

"Now what the hell goes on here?" Cole said. "You." He pointed at Barker. "You do the talking. We'll come to the rest of you."

"He was . . . hanging," Barker said, "a rope around his neck. He was hanging"—he gestured—"from that beam, a chair kicked away beneath him, and the other end of the rope attached there, to one of the hooks of that fireplace. He was hanging like that, dead."

"You all saw him?"

"Yes. Most of us."

"Hanging like you described?"

"Yes."

"Who discovered him?"

"My daughter," Ethel said, holding Sara closely.

"What time?"

"About . . . about midnight," Sara said weakly.

"Then?"

"We got the women away," Barker said. "There was a note in his pocket, a suicide note."

"Where is it?"

"In the desk drawer."

"I thought you said nothing was touched. Somebody said that."

"That was the only thing we touched," Barker said.

"Who touched it?"

"I. Only I."

Bruce Lawson interrupted. "May I say something, Chief?"

"What is it?"

"I took photos. Used up five rolls of film. I told you my business, and I'm an expert in my field. I'll get the film for you. You can get them back to town and have them developed in a hurry, and you'll have a clear picture of . . . of . . . before . . ." He pointed at the body in bewilderment.

"Where's this film?"

"In my room."

"Okay, get that stuff down here. You're excused for that purpose, Mr. Lawson."

Bruce hurried out.

"You can look the body over now," Cole said to Dr. York. To Barker he said, "You sure he was hanging there when you saw him last?"

"Oh, of course."

"Tell me what happened, exactly what happened?"

Barker told him all of it, the discovery of the body, the reading of the suicide note, Lawson's taking of the photographs, his closing the door with orders that no one go in, the fact that the phones were dead, our going off to get to the police and the fact that the bridge was down, our return with the injured Nick.

He was a good man, Cole. He hit where it was open. "Four men went to the bridge?"

"Yes."

"The women were all upstairs?"

"Yes."

"That left you and Mr. Duff?"

"Yes."

"Were either of you apart during that time?"

"No, as a matter of fact, we weren't. We were both wearing bathrobes at the time. We went up to change into clothes. His room is directly opposite mine. Our doors were open and we were talking as we dressed. None of the women could have come down either, or we'd have seen them. When

93

we were dressed, we came down together. No one entered this study, there's no question about that."

"What time did you people shut up shop here?"

"It was about two-thirty."

"What time did you open up shop again?"

"About seven."

"That means that this body was taken down some time during the night—between two-thirty last night and about seven this morning."

"Yes. That's it. No question."

"What do you think, Mr. Duff?"

"I agree with Mr. Barker," Duff said.

Bruce came into the room, running. "It's gone!"

"What? What's gone? What the hell goes on here?"

"All of it! Gone! My camera, all the film—*gone!*"

Cole rubbed a hand across his face. "Now what the hell!"

"I don't understand this, any of it. First"—he gestured toward where the doctor was working over Freddie—"first somebody fooling around with a dead body, and now my camera—"

"Just a minute, young man," Cole shouted.

"Yes, sir."

"Calm down."

"Yes, sir."

"Where'd you have that camera and those films?"

"I'd put them back in my suitcase."

"In your room?"

"Yes, sir."

"Lock the suitcase?"

"No, sir. I didn't see any reason—"

"Yes, yes, perfectly natural. Now, were you in your room all night?"

"Yes, sir. Until Mr. Barker woke me this morning."

"Were you asleep?"

"Yes, sir."

"Fall asleep right away?"

"No, sir. I tossed around a good bit. I'd say I fell asleep about three, three-thirty."

"So that some time after that it figures someone stole that stuff—"

"But why? Why the dickens should anybody—"

"I wish I knew. This is a hell of a note." Cole turned to Barker. "Here's a thing that figures for a simple suicide. So it gets complicated with matters *after* the fact." He went to the doctor who had straightened up. "What have we got, Doc?"

"Quick look, death by strangulation. Autopsy ought to corroborate that. Vertebrae intact, no broken neck. Rope marks very clear on the neck. One curious thing, though."

"Yes?"

"There's a bruise on the left cheekbone."

"That's got nothing to do with any of this," Barker said.

"Hasn't it?" Cole said. "How do you know?"

"Because I did it," Nick said.

"*You* did it?"

"I boffed him."

"When?"

"Yesterday evening. We had a little battle. He'd been picking on me all day."

"Battle? You and your boss? What about?"

Nick hesitated.

Barker said, "Chief."

"What about?" Cole insisted.

"He claimed," Nick said haltingly, "claimed I wasn't paying enough attention to Linda."

"Linda?"

"Miss Moreno."

"Chief," Barker said. "I want to talk to you alone please." Cole wrinkled his face querulously. "I insist," Barker said and took him by the arm and they encamped in the kitchen.

We murmured, moved about, sat down, stood up, grabbed a nibble of brandy here and there. The Chief would be a wiser man, I was certain, after his conference with Barker. He was probably being briefed on the idiosyncrasies of genius, beards, doxies, and the unorthodoxies of love amidst greasepaint.

He returned a grimmer man. He looked curiously at Linda, curiously at Nick, curiously at Tony, curiously at Ethel, curiously at Suzy, curiously at Janet, curiously at me. He sighed as though he were trying to keep back a belch. Then he said, of all things: "Now what's this about your finger, young man?"

"Can your doctor look at it, please?"

"Sure, take him upstairs, Doc."

"Yes, sir." Nick and the doctor left the room.

"Okay," Cole said. "Now let's get a little system into things around here. I want all of you to go up to your rooms and stay there. I'll question each of you individually." As we started to shuffle out, he said, "Except you, Mr. Barker. And Chambers and Lawson. After all, I want to keep the criminal investigators right here near me—one of them may come up with a real bright big-city idea." And when the rest of them were out of the room, he said, "Where's that suicide note, Mr. Barker?"

"In the desk drawer."

"And you're the only one who touched it?"

"Yes, sir."

"Then you get it for me, please." Barker got it. "Lay it on the desk, please." Barker laid it. Cole read it. "Well, at least *that's* uncomplicated." He drew a large wallet from an inside pocket. "Place it in here, Mr. Barker," he said. Barker did. "Thank you," Cole said. "Our little laboratory will give us the word on it." He put the wallet away. "We'll have a fingerprint man here soon, and the whole household will be printed. According to rights, yours should show on that note, and those of the deceased." He turned to me. "How'd I do, Mr. Detective?" he inquired sardonically.

"Couldn't have done better myself," I said, and I meant it.

"Well, thank you grandly," he said, and perhaps he meant it. "Flanagan!" he said to one of his men.

"Yes, sir," Flanagan said.

"Do your duty as an undertaker. Get this body out of here and arrange for the autopsy. Afterward, we'll probably ship it to New York. I'll talk to the widow." Flanagan and another man went to the body. "And Flanagan," Cole said.

"Yes, sir?"

"When you get back to town, deliver a message to my staff. Tell them I want every one of them out here—pronto. Every one of them."

"Yes, sir," Flanagan said.

And then Freddie was carried out to the hearse.

"Okay, now, you three," Cole said. "Before I go up to question the others. Which one of you saw Mr. Flanders last?"

"Well," I said, "now I don't approve, Chief. That's asking a multiple question, in a sense. How the hell do we know which one of us saw him last? We haven't consulted on it."

"Let's put it this way, Chief," Barker said. "Freddie went in here, into this study, at about seven-thirty. I think we can all agree on that."

"Yes," Lawson said.

"Yes," I said.

"Okay, pardon me," Cole said. "Now, did you see him after that, Mr. Chambers?"

"No, sir," I said. "Not till Sara started screaming. Not until he was dead."

"Me neither," Lawson said.

"Which means that neither of you was in this room until his suicide was discovered. Correct?"

"Yes," we said.

"How about you, Mr. Barker?"

"I went in here at eight-fifteen yesterday evening."

"Eight-fifteen? How can you be so precise?"

"I looked at my watch, Mr. Cole. That's how I can be so precise."

"He was alive?"

96

"Very much so."

"Why'd you go in?"

"I asked him if he wanted something to eat. He said he didn't."

"What was his mood?"

"Irascible. Also drunk. Quite drunk."

"Would you say it was a suicidal mood?"

"I don't know what a suicidal mood is," Barker said. "He was angry, fretting, troubled, drunk. But that was not unusual for Freddie Flanders."

"Okay, so we know definitely he was alive at eight-fifteen. What did you do then, Mr. Barker?"

"Went up to bed. These two gentlemen had preceded me."

Cole paced about. "All right, let's switch it now. He's been found dead, and all the rest of it. This household then bedded down at about two-thirty. Lawson's already told us he was asleep until you woke him. What about you, Mr. Barker?"

"Fell asleep almost at once. I was awakened at about six by Mr. Chambers telling me the phones were in order again and that he had gotten through to you."

"What about you, Chambers? From two-thirty to six?"

"I was in my room, hitting the phone every fifteen minutes. Suzy Lyons was with me."

"All night?" said Adam Cole, eyebrows arching.

"Don't look so prurient, Chief," I said.

"What's prurient?" the Chief said.

"That young lady was in my room to keep me company."

"What else?" he said ingenuously.

"You keep looking like that, Chiefie," I said.

"Like what?" he said.

"Prurient," I said. "Like you think something naughty was going on. After all, I kept hitting that phone every fifteen minutes."

"So what?" the Chief said. "You're a young fella. How long does it take?"

"Oh, no, Chiefie," I said.

He got crunchy again, like a stalk of celery. "Okay," he said. "Flanders was alive at eight-fifteen. At midnight he was hanging. Now you three deny leaving your rooms and taking him down. Let's get that categorically."

"You've got it," we said.

I said, "There's another thing, Chief. This will help. I woke Mr. Barker at six. From six onward, I was in and out of my room, the door was open, I was checking with Suzy, things like that."

"What the hell's that mean?" Cole said.

"It means that nobody could have gone into this room,

taken him down, left the room with the rope, all that jazz —without my hearing or seeing. So I'm giving you a time period on that. Whatever happened happened between two-thirty and six. That's pretty definite."

"Unless you did it," he said.

"That's right," I said.

"Well, thanks anyway," he said. "Now you three can stay here. I'm going up to question the people. Come on, Maney."

Maney, the man who had been taking notes, went with him.

TWENTY-ONE

THE FIRST ONES back were Dr. Frank York and Nick Wallace. Nick was as pale as a frightened bridegroom but he was grinning just as gamely. "I got preference," Nick said. "I got questioned first."

"I'm taking Mr. Wallace to the hospital," Dr. York said.

"Where's the hospital?" I said.

"Dover's Notch," Dr. York said, "about ten miles west of Rexville."

"Hospital?" Barker looked worried, his eyes moving to Nick's finger, out of the sling now, but thickly bandaged.

"I don't believe in keeping the facts from my patients," Dr. York said. "That's a badly mangled finger and there's a smashed bone. There was a good deal of coagulation and I had to cut it and bleed it before I put in the penicillin. There's a possibility that there may be an amputation to the first knuckle. Nothing serious, but nasty."

"Sorry, Nickie," Barker said and went to him and hugged him.

"What the hell," Nickie said. "Rather lose a piece of finger than lose a job. And I did get my job back, didn't I?"

"Damn right you did," Barker said.

York was at the phone. "Mike," he said into the phone. "Mike, listen. Flanagan will be in with a dead boy and a message. The message is that the Chief wants the whole danged staff up here. Now hold that. Wait until I come in with a Nick Wallace. You'll take his prints, and then you'll come up here, all of you. And don't forget to take that portable fingerprint deal with you. Yes, I'm leaving right now." He hung up and he said to Nick, "Let's go, young man."

"Happy landings," I said.

"Thanks," Nick said.

"Doctor," Barker said.

"Yes?" the doctor said.

"How's Sara Flanders?" Barker said. "Did you look in on her?"

98

"Yes, I did," the doctor said. "Terribly affected, that young lady. I administered sedation, but not enough to knock her out. She'll be groggy, but Cole will be able to question her. I left some pills with her mother for afterward. Now come along, Mr. Wallace."

Nick waved, grinned, and followed the doctor.

"Lousy break," Lawson said, and then pricked up as Cole came in with Linda Moreno. Linda was wearing a simple black knitted dress but pressed to Linda's audacious curves the simple black knitted dress lost all its simplicity and became very intricate indeed. Even Cole's deputies pricked up.

"Miss Moreno, it appears," Cole said, "was the last person to see Mr. Flanders alive. I prefer that she tell her story here before witnesses."

Although I was tempted, I did not say, "Hear! Hear!"

"Please sit down, Miss Moreno," Cole said.

Linda sat and crossed her legs.

Lawson and Cole deputies pricked up further. Even old Cole pricked. "Miss Moreno," he said, "you came down into this study at about a quarter to nine last night? Right?"

"Yes. That's right. I did." A blast of brandy accompanied Linda's words. Linda, like I, must have brought her own bottle, and Linda was under strain. Linda would not be lapping it up so early in the morning were she not under strain.

"Quarter to nine last night," Cole said. "Why did you come down?"

"I wanted to talk to him alone, that's why."

"Why?"

"He'd been after me all day, insulting me. He'd had that fight with Nick, because of me. This young man, Bruce Lawson, I like him and I'm not ashamed to admit it. Freddie didn't like that, but Freddie was entitled to have it happen right under his nose."

"Why?" Cole said.

"That's exactly what I came down to talk to him about."

"What?" Cole said.

"He'd invited me here. He'd also brought Ethel out. He had a hell of a nerve and he knew it. How much did that bum think he could get away with?"

"Nice way to talk of the dead," I said.

"I'm no hypocrite," she said. "I don't care that he's dead."

"Did you kill him?" Cole said.

"Oh now stop it. I didn't kill anybody. *He* did."

"*What?*" Cole said.

"May I have a drink, please? Brandy, please?"

One of the deputies went to the bar.

"What do you want with it?" Cole said.

"Just a glass," Linda said.

I took the bottle and poured an adequate dose for Linda. "Thank you," she said to me and smiled at Bruce Lawson. "Who killed who?" Cole demanded.

"I came down here to have it out with him for mixing me into a thing with his wife and daughter. I asked him didn't he have respect for me, or for his wife. He told me to mind my goddamned business and that he'd told his wife to mind her goddamned business when she'd brought this very thing up to him some time during the day. He told me he had troubles of his own, that he'd killed a man—"

"What man?" Cole said.

I made a mental note to use Linda as corroboration in my story to Parker. After all, Cole's deputy was making notes, and this was part of the record.

"What man?" Cole said.

"He didn't say what man. He just said it. Freddie was a guy who could say all kinds of things when he was drinking and, brother, Freddie was drinking. I didn't pay it any mind. I had a beef, and I wanted to air my beef. But it was no use. He was just too damned drunk to handle. I got out of there and went up to sleep."

"What time?" Cole said.

"Nine o'clock."

Cole looked about, at all of us. "That's the final word on it. Nobody saw Mr. Flanders alive after that. That suicide happened between nine and midnight. Thank you very much, Miss Moreno."

She stood up, glass in hand.

"May I take her up?" Bruce Lawson said.

"Go right ahead, young fella," Cole said. "If I wasn't a married man, I'd say I envy you."

That brought a burst of appreciative laughter from his deputies. He waited until Bruce and Linda had departed and then he inquired: "Well, what do you think, Mr. Barker?"

"Think of what?" Barker said.

"This whole bit," Cole said. "All of it. Do you think Mr. Flanders committed suicide?"

"Absolutely," Barker said. "He wrote that note. I know his handwriting. He committed suicide."

"For what reason?"

"That I wouldn't know."

"What about his being taken down? Any theories on that?"

"Yes," Barker said slowly. "I think that somebody in this household, somehow, for some reason, considered it—how shall I say—wrong, indecent, for a man to hang like that . . ."

"Good. Good, Mr. Barker," Cole said. "That seems reasonable enough. How about the disappearance of the camera and the film? Have you given that any thought?"

"Yes, I have," Barker said.

"I'd appreciate your opinion," Cole said.

"Perhaps there was something on Freddie, something I didn't notice," Barker said, "something that might show in the pictures, something that might be embarrassing to somebody, even to Freddie, that that somebody didn't want the world to see."

"Interesting theory," Cole said. "What do you think they did with that film and camera? Stow them away somewhere here in the house?"

"That would be idiotic, don't you think?"

"Yes, I think. In fact I'm doing my thinking with you as a sounding board and I'm grateful for your co-operation. What *do* you think?"

"I think they were gotten rid of outside," Barker said. "With all that snow and wind out there, we couldn't hear a car drive up or drive away. With all the chasms, ravines and gorges hereabouts—sheer drops of hundreds of feet— the person rips up the films and then tosses the whole kit and caboodle overboard, and they're gone, probably forever."

"Now what about the rope, Mr. Barker? Evidently, that's gone too. How does that fit in with your theory, sir?"

"It doesn't," Barker said.

"Any ideas on that?"

"On that I'm completely baffled," Barker said.

TWENTY-TWO

S o WAS everybody else.

The rope did not show up. Neither did the camera or the film.

When Cole's staff arrived, an augmented staff of twenty-five men, fingerprints were taken, and then a minute and expert search was made of the house and grounds, the garage, the cars, the surrounding premises.

Total: nothing.

Cole finally threw up his hands in disgust. "Whoever did it, and why the hell he ever did it, none of us will ever know. No use banging your head against a stone wall. I got no objection to you folks going back to New York. There'll be an inquest in a week or so—we'll set it on a Sunday because you people are show people and there's no show on Sunday. That was Mr. Barker's idea, and I wish to thank Mr. Barker for everything, he has been of great help. That's about it, folks. We're getting out of here now. Good bye, all."

Barker was in sole charge again, as we started packing. He came up to my room and he said, "We've got to allocate as to how we go back."

"Come again?" I said.

"We had five cars, coming here, with thirteen people including the cook. We're not going back the same way, I mean, the same groups as came up."

"Freddie's not going at all," I said.

"Never thought he'd end that way," Barker said somberly. He shook his heavy shoulders, went to the phone. He called the hospital at Dover's Notch. He inquired about Nick Wallace. He put his hand over the mouthpiece and smiling he called to me, "I'm going to talk to him." Then he was back on the phone, saying, "Yes, Nickie. How are you?" He listened, interposed a few words, then he said, "All right. Stay put, and rest. We'll have someone pick you up." He hung up and he said, "What do you know?"

"What?" I said, stuffing clothes into a bag.

"They amputated up to the first joint of the index finger, but already he's up and around and feeling fine and wanting to go home. He has full permission to leave. One of us will pick him up. Now let's see. Sara'll have to be with Ethel, and I'll drive Freddie's car . . ."

The way it worked out Joel Barker drove Freddie's car which contained Ethel and Sara. Tony's station wagon took him, Linda and the cook. Janet drove Barker's car and her passenger was Duff. I drove Suzy. That left Bruce Lawson to whom Barker had said, "I'd appreciate it if you'd pick up Nickie at Dover's Notch. Are you in any hurry?"

"No, not at all, sir."

"Then stall around a while. The more he rests there before the trip, the better I'd like it. I'll leave you the keys and you can lock up. You can return the keys to me at my office when you get back. I hope you don't mind."

"No, sir, not at all," Bruce said. "Glad to be of help."

When we got back to town, I dropped Suzy off, went home and went to sleep. I slept all the way around the clock. Twenty-four hours later, when Duff called me—that woke me up.

TWENTY-THREE

THE PHONE BATTERED at my dreams like an anxious psychiatrist. It shrilled like a termagant. It pealed like the panegyric of a press agent. It was as ceaseless as the importunities of the tax collector. I reached out a limp hand, brought the receiver to a throbbing ear, said, "Good bye, please."

"This is Edward Duff," said Edward Duff.

"Thrilling," I said. "Good bye."

"It's six o'clock."

"Great," I said. "Good bye."

"In the evening," he said.

"Evening?" I said and sat up and began to take notice.

"I didn't want to bother you," he said. "I purposely waited until evening. You were up most of yesterday. Would you like to have dinner?"

"How's about eight o'clock at Nino's?"

"Wonderful," he said. "Where is it?"

"Fifty-second Street. East. You better call for reservations."

"Wonderful," he said.

Nino's was warm, cozy, expensive and food-smelling. The lights made princesses of the women, and the men looked as though they had checked their white chargers outside. Even I, gazing at my unhappy reflection in the mirror at the bar, looked only slightly shopworn. I was early, and I experimented with some of the vitamins recommended by Mrs. Dee Dunstan Millay: side-cars. I do not know about the vitamins but I must say that side-cars before breakfast do more for the inner man, somehow, than orange juice. I was a-glow with expectation when Duff arrived.

"Nothing like a good long sleep," he said. "You look fine."

"God bless vitamins," I said. "Let's have breakfast."

"Dinner," he said.

"Okay," I said. "Be stubborn."

Duff had a fancy dish. I had steak, large, thick and rare. It sat well over the side-cars. After three cups of coffee I felt human enough to risk chocolate mousse. It was divine. I sat back and smoked and expanded. I was ready for whatever was on Duff's mind.

"You think we ought to get it over with?" he said.

"What?" I said.

"Allan Sylvester," he said.

"Want to talk about Freddie?" I said.

"No," he said.

"Crazy thing about that rope and camera and films," I said.

"I've got my own worries," he said.

"Where's Katy?" I said.

"Rather safely away," he said and smiled.

"Let me make a call," I said.

I called downtown to Parker. He was busy on another wire, would I wait? Yes, I would wait. I sighed as I waited.

The hours of public detectives were as weird as the hours of private detectives. I got the inevitable ear-splitting click and then I got Parker.

"Parker," he said. "Yes?"

"Pete Chambers."

"Hi, Pete."

"You going to be in a while?"

"Yessir. Crime's slack. I'm sitting around bored to tears."

"I'll un-bore you, Pappy. Hear about Freddie Flanders?"

"Who hasn't? The papers are full of it. Where've you been?"

"Sleeping," I said. "Wait for me, will you? I've got some news."

"I'll be waiting, laddie."

Back at the table, I hustled Duff into action. He paid, I offered him my share, he waved it off, and we quit Nino's. Outside I said, "We'd better stop off for the affidavits."

"I've got them with me," he said.

"Smart fella," I said. "Let's walk a bit and sort of refresh our story."

"Nothing to refresh, really," Duff said as we strolled. "I'm going to tell the entire truth, except that neither you nor Zangwill Manchester were ever at her apartment."

"How about that key Sylvester had?" I said.

"What about it?" he said.

"Katy gave him a key?" I said.

"Yes," he said dismally. "Katy had given him a key."

I switched off that quickly. "There are some other items for the cops, other than the affidavits. There are Sylvester's belongings."

"I've got them all," he said, "wrapped in Sylvester's very own handkerchief."

"Where?" I said.

"In the car," he said.

"And where's the car?" I said.

"Parked right in front of Nino's restaurant," he said.

"So why are we walking this way?" I said.

"Let's walk back," he said.

When we got into the car, I said, "With the one exception you mentioned, I'm going to have to tell the entire truth too. That includes Havana. All of it. That's the part, of course, that ties Freddie in. How're you going to feel about that?"

"It's perfectly all right with me," he said. "It had been my intention to wait a much longer time before going to the police. But after what you learned from Mr. Flanders, I think the sooner we make a complete breast of all of it, the better. I'm going to plead for Katy, of course, plead to

104

keep her out of it. And there's no reason why she should be publicly involved now. Sylvester's death is already out of the newspapers. If the police have that case solved, that is that; certainly there's no need for publicity on it."

"Possibly, there might be," I said.

"If there is, there is," he said.

Detective-lieutenant Louis Parker, after the first amenities, hardly spoke a word. After I had introduced Duff, and introduced the subject matter, he had called in a police stenographer, and then we were on our own. I gave him Part One: how Duff had retained me that Tuesday upon the recommendation of Agatha Levine. Duff gave him Part Two: how he had gone to his daughter's apartment that evening, what he had found, what he had done, and why.

At this point we produced Sylvester's effects. Duff showed Parker the clip from the automatic and expressed his reasons why he had known that Sylvester had been murdered and had not been a suicide.

Parker grunted.

I took up Part Three.

"Somehow," I said, "my client seemed obsessed with the idea that his daughter was involved with Sylvester. I didn't have the faintest notion as to why."

"Of course not," Parker said down his nose. "Not the faintest."

"But really not, Lieutenant," I said.

"Who said different, Detective?" he said.

"Mr. Duff wanted me to continue my researches as regarded his daughter, with a special point to possibly proving that she had nothing to do with the murder of Allan Sylvester."

"And you weren't even curious as to why?" Parker said.

"Well, he *had* informed me that Katy and Sylvester had been pretty close, that the guy *did* have a key to the kid's apartment."

"So?" Parker said.

I told him about the party at Flanders' home that night, Suzy's picking up Katy at the airport, my sending Katy to her father. I told him that it was decided that I go down to Havana to do a check there. I told him the entire Havana story.

That is when Duff produced the affidavits.

Parker read them, read them into the record, put them down, said, "Go on."

Then I told him all about the vacation at Freddie's Lodge.

Now Parker put fire to his cigar. "Mr. Chambers," he said for the record, "you had been down to see me about Sylvester's death. You said you were talking to me on behalf of a client and that that was confidential. Was Mr. Edward Duff that client?"

"Yes, sir."

"Thank you, Mr. Duff," Parker said, "although I appreciate the motives for your actions, and though I must admit that I respect those motives, you must realize that such actions may constitute a crime. Your coming here now voluntarily, of course, mitigates in your favor. However, I am only a policeman, and this is a matter for the District Attorney. Will you be present at the District Attorney's office tomorrow at two o'clock?"

"Yes, sir," Duff said.

"You too, Mr. Chambers?" Parker said.

"Yes, sir, Lieutenant Parker," I said.

Duff said, "Please, lieutenant. If there is any way in the world to keep my daughter's name out of this—I don't mean out of the official hearings—but out of the newspapers, away from public scandal—I beseech you . . ."

"I'll do whatever *I* can," Parker said. "The fact that she's under eighteen will certainly be taken into consideration."

"You can check," I said, "with Havana. You can check Flanders' vouchers. You can check with the Rexville records that Linda Moreno stated that Flanders had told her that he had killed a man—"

"Don't tell me what to check, Mr. Chambers," Parker said for the record.

"A thousand pardons," I said for the same record. "Of course the lieutenant knows his business. May I add another point, if you please?"

"Certainly, Mr. Chambers."

"I believe," I said for the record, "that we may have here the motive for Flanders' suicide. This man confessed to me that he had committed murder. He thought he could get away with it. Maybe, legally, he could get away with it. But perhaps his conscience reared up, perhaps he couldn't square murder with his own conscience, perhaps in his drunken state, overwhelmed with the enormity of what he had done . . ."

"You have a point there, Mr. Chambers." Parker stood up. "All right," he said. "Anything else?"

There was nothing else.

Parker dismissed the stenographer. He requested that Duff wait outside. Then he marched into his office, backhanded an affectionate slap at my head, and sat down again. He was elaborate in lighting a fresh cigar. Then he said, "All right, laddie, let's hear it."

"Off the record," I said. "Or on?"

"Off," he said. "Just between Pappy and laddie."

I told him, the whole *megilla*, including Zangwill Man-

106

chester and the knock on the head with the candlestick.

He chuckled approvingly. "That's more like it," he said. "Off the record, of course."

"I couldn't let it stay that way, *on* the record?"

"Why not?"

"Obstructing justice is okay for a father protecting an under-age daughter, I mean this kind of by-the-letter-but-not-in-the-spirit obstructing justice. But a private richard is such by virtue of a license granted by the State, and the State might be unhappy when the richard gets human and plays ball like a human being."

"You got to hand it to the guy," Parker said, "off the record."

"Duff?"

"Yeah. Took nerve. It may work out. Baxter won't be unsympathetic, he's got three daughters of his own. Plus I'll tell it most sympathetically. Cops are human too. Even D.A.'s. I'll see you at two o'clock tomorrow."

Duff went home, and I went to Suzy's place, and two o'clock the next day I showed up at the District Attorney's office wearing the same clothes but with a fresh shave. The D.A. was busy, but Parker had affidavits for Duff and me to sign, which we did. "Everything checked out," Parker said, "including Havana, the hospital there, the Millays, Flanders' cancelled voucher, and Linda Moreno's statement to the Rexville authorities, and we got an affidavit on it right here from her. I talked with the Commissioner, gave him the whole deal, and our book is closed on Sylvester. Nobody's looking for great credit on it, and there are no announcements to the press. If it ever comes up though, we'll tell them who and what, and they can do as they please. Won't come up though, I don't think. There's absolutely no interest in that small-time punk, none whatsoever."

"Have you talked to the D.A.?" I asked.

"He's got the whole story. He's human."

Then we were called in. Baxter shook hands with Duff, said, "You're in a pickle but it's not too great a pickle. Your coming in voluntarily, plus the fact that the murder is actually solved, all of that doesn't hurt." He smiled. "However, it is not up to me to pardon the ways of the transgressor. In fact, my function is quite the contrary. However, I do not indict. That is the function of the Grand Jury. The Grand Jury is in session right now, and I have an appointment to present the facts. Come along, gentlemen, and please don't be too nervous. There are immensely human mitigating circumstances here, and I shall certainly recite them in my presentation. Grand Juries are human too."

"Everybody's human." Parker grinned. "That's all I've been

hearing. Sweetness and light and everybody's human. We sound like characters in a Saroyan play."

But we *were* all human, damn it, weren't we?

I was human.

Duff was human.

The policeman was human.

The District Attorney was human.

The Grand Jury, as it turned out, was human too. It refused to indict. In fact, it dismembered into individuals who shook hands with Duff and sat around and chatted. Katy Duff was a hundred percent in the clear. Edward Duff had taken some extreme steps in his capacity as a father and he was practically a hero for it. Peter Chambers had earned six thousand dollars—aside from expenditure to Zang—for doing few things more than taking a vacation in Havana and taking a second vacation at Freddie's Lodge. People were human! Sweetness and light! The Daring Young Man On The Flying Trapeze! The Time Of Your Life! The Beautiful People! Hooray for Saroyan! Hello Out There, Willie!

TWENTY-FOUR

BUT FREDDIE FLANDERS was quite dead and his inquest took place that very Sunday. We played a return engagement at the county seat of Rexville, all of us with the exception of Sara. Sara's condition had worsened and she was in a sanitorium under the care of one of the top psychiatrists in the city. Temporarily, Joel Barker was paying the bills.

The inquest was handled briskly and all the facts were quickly brought out. The suicide note was shown to the jury and an expert's testimony proclaimed that the only fingerprints thereon were Freddie's and Barker's, and the jury was informed as to why Barker's fingerprints were on the note. The note had an indentation in one corner that could have been made by a fingernail, but this was not unusual on any sheet of paper, and was of no consequence. It was proven, beyond a vestige of a doubt, that the note was in Freddie's handwriting. Medical testimony, bolstered by postmortem findings, showed conclusively that death had ensued by strangulation. Expert police testimony made it manifest that such strangulation had been by rope, that no hands had touched the throat. Further autopsy findings, perhaps needless in the circumstances, disclosed that Freddie had had a very damp evening, that he had been thoroughly, wringing-wet, hell-bent-for-election, cock-eyed drunk.

The coroner's jury brought in a verdict of death by suicide, although the record specifically contained mention of the jury's bewilderment relative to the events that followed:

the taking down of the body, and the disappearance of the rope, camera and films.

When it was over, and the others were having coffee before the trip back, I buttonholed the deputy named Maney and I inquired if there were photostatic copies of the suicide note.

"Plenty," he said. "Why?"

"I'd like to have one."

"You'd like to have one? Why?"

"Freddie Flanders was my best friend. I loved him like a brother. I would like to have the very last thing he had ever written, even though it's only a photostat. Maybe I'm a sentimental kind of guy. You said you got plenty. I hope you can spare one. It's worth fifty bucks to me."

It was a long speech but the last sentence accomplished the point.

He brought me a copy and I said, "Thank you."

"You're welcome," he said as he took my money.

Freddie's will was probated and made public, and the newspapers played it up on two counts. First was the fact that a playwright had accumulated fifteen million dollars in twenty-five years of success, of which five million was in actual cash in vaults, and the balance was in real estate and gilt-edged bonds. Second, some of the clauses in the will were sufficiently bizarre to warrant newspaper space. There were four specific bequests: $500,000 to his wife Ethel Flanders; $500,000 to his daughter Sara Flanders; $200,000 to his partner Joel Barker; $200,000 to his friend Linda Moreno. After the distribution of these bequests, the remainder of the estate was to be divided equally between his wife and daughter. But there were two clauses of modification, and they were both interesting. The first—after stating that his wife was to serve as executrix and that he had no debts—ordered that the cash bequests be paid within one week of the probate of the will. There was the posthumous advice that the testator, all his life, had felt that people had to wait far too long to receive bequests when they were mentioned in wills. If the Courts raised any question as to this clause, it was ordered that the executrix post bond for the amount of the bequests in total—but that the bequests be paid nonetheless within the first week of probate. The second clause modified the specific bequest to Linda Moreno. It stated, simply, that in the event that the decease of the testator eventuated by reason of his murder—no matter how or by whom he was murdered—then the bequest to Linda Moreno was null and void, and that the amount then fall into the residual portion of the estate.

There was a good deal of tittering in theatrical circles. Good old Freddie. As he had threatened, so had he done. He had often proclaimed the contents of his will, his one curb upon the torrid temper of the tempestuous Linda Moreno—the clause involving her was his insurance that she would not over-reach herself when striking back against the whip of his nagging and needling.

After many conferences between lawyers and Surrogate, the terms of the will were complied with, and within a week Freddie Flanders' testamentary flights of fancy faded from the public prints.

Somehow, nobody missed him.

And everybody seemed to have gained something by his demise.

The house on Sixty-second Street fell back into routine. Sara, after therapy which included shock treatment, came home, more quiet, more shy than ever. Ethel resumed her quiet customary way of life, but Edward Duff, of all people, became a constant caller, and he and Ethel were seen together about town. *Flesh and Fury* continued triumphant, but with a new star. Linda Moreno had been fired—without cause, she said; with cause, said management—and Equity had set a date for a hearing on the matter. Janet Lewis was now the star of *Flesh and Fury*, and Joel Barker, now sole protagonist of Flanders and Barker, was reading new plays for the new season. Nick Wallace was promoted to permanent press agent for all Flanders and Barker enterprises, at a raise in salary. Linda Moreno did not appear at all distressed about the momentary set-back in her career. On the contrary, gay and more beautiful than ever, she and Bruce Lawson were a blazingly handsome couple, doing the town every night. Bruce had a new and elegantly furnished apartment on East Seventy-ninth Street, and a sleek new car, and the malice-mongers made much of the fact that Linda's latest young swain had come into all of his new splendor coincident with the time that dear Linda had fallen heir to Freddie's largesse. And Tony Royal, impenetrable and impassive as ever, continued as smiling host of Royal House which was doing capacity business as usual.

Everybody was happy except me.

Suzy Lyons had given me the air.

TWENTY-FIVE

Suddenly she was not in when I called. Suddenly she was not calling me. Suddenly she no longer went to Royal House. Suddenly I realized I was making a nuisance of myself trying to get in touch with her. So I stopped making a nuisance of myself. I carried my torch like a gentleman, working by day, tippling by night. I was a steady customer at Royal House, entering swacked and emerging swackier, but no one said me nay, least of all Tony Royal. It went on for three weeks, and then on this cold, drear, winter-rainy night, as I sat alone at a corner table at two in the morning, I felt a familiar warmth at my thigh, and there she was squeezed close to me, saying, "I'm glad you're here. I couldn't hold out any longer."

"What happened?" I said.

"You're a bastard," she said. "I never thought of you as a bastard. I couldn't keep going with you thinking you're a bastard. That's what happened," she said and smiled at Tony who had come over and seated himself opposite us.

"Joint's a morgue, ain't it?" Tony said. Royal House had very few customers. Of the regulars, only Linda Moreno and Bruce Lawson were present seated upon a banquette on the opposite wall. Bruce, looking up, now saw Suzy and he waved like he was flagging down a slow-moving train. Suzy waved in return.

"What do you expect on a night like this?" I asked of Tony. "This kind of night you get the torch-bearers and the drunks."

"He's been both," Tony said to Suzy.

"I love him," Suzy said.

"Sure. You've been proving it to him real great. Women," he said and sighed and snapped his fingers for a waiter. "What are you drinking, Miss Lyons?"

"I drink champagne when I celebrate," Suzy said.

"You celebrating?" Tony said.

"I'm celebrating," Suzy said.

"Champagne," Tony said to the waiter. "And don't charge it to this table. Charge it to Cupid."

"Who he?" asked the waiter.

"Me," Tony said.

"Oh," said the waiter.

"Well, go away," Tony said to the waiter. "Go get the champagne, for Chrissake."

"It's only I don't get with this cupid-bit. That's some kinda baby-doll, ain't it?" the waiter said.

"Please go away," Tony said. The waiter went. Tony sighed. "It just ain't my night," Tony said.

"It's mine," I said.

"Enjoy yourself," Tony said. "Me, I'm getting out of this morgue. I'm going over to the Copa Lounge where there's maybe a little action."

"Action?" I said. "Or torch?"

"Torch? Torch for what?"

I raised my eyebrows and pointed with my nose. At Linda Moreno.

"Brother," Tony said, "maybe you're a little psychic. I did

111

figure the bounce from Freddie would land her back to me. So that beautiful hunk of man had to get in the way." He shrugged and stood up. "Bye now, kiddies. Have fun. There's nothing like making up."

"Why a bastard?" I said when we were alone.

"Protecting your client. For six thousand bucks."

"Duff?" I said.

"Who else?" she said.

"What the hell are you talking about?"

"Freddie Flanders."

"Freddie Flanders?" I said. "For that I got three weeks of solitary confinement?"

The waiter brought the champagne, opened it, poured, said, "It's on baby-doll," and went away.

"Freddie Flanders was murdered," she said.

"You think so?" I said.

"I think so," she said.

"I think so too," I said. "You think Duff murdered him?"

"You didn't do anything about it."

"Whatever I didn't do—it wasn't because of Duff."

"Honest and truly?"

"Cross my cotton-pickin' heart."

"Then I'm glad I'm here," she said and drank champagne. "I thought it was because of Duff, and I couldn't face you to ask you, to talk about it, because if it turned out because of Duff, I'd die of disappointment in you. I'm glad I'm here. I'm a big dope, but I do love you." She drank more champagne and set the glass away. "Why do you think Freddie was murdered?"

"I didn't start this, baby. You did."

"I think Freddie was murdered," she said, "simply because Freddie wasn't the type to commit suicide. Period. Furthermore, he had nothing to commit suicide about."

"He killed Sylvester. You know the whole story."

"And that was crap you gave the cops about his conscience and you know it."

"Yes," I said, "I know it."

"Why do you think Freddie was murdered?"

"Same reason as you. Plus the crazy shenanigans afterward."

"So why didn't you try to do something about it? It's in your line of business."

"Honey," I said, "if Freddie was murdered, somebody in that house murdered him—"

"Including Duff?"

"Including Duff. Anyway, if he was murdered, somebody in that house murdered him, and there were a lot of nice people in that house—"

112

"A murderer is not nice people. That was the way I was brought up to think."

"Look, a coroner's jury in the county seat of Rexville declared his death a suicide. The cops, the authorities up there, say it's suicide. Where do I come off, sticking my nose in, and why, and what could I accomplish?"

"I don't know," she said dismally. "I really don't know. Did you do *anything* about it?"

"Only this," I said. I brought out my wallet and showed her the photostatic copy of the suicide note.

"Why?" she said.

"I don't know why," I said. "There's something about that note that touches a chord in my unconscious."

"What?"

"I don't know what?" I said and I put it away. "Maybe it'll come to me, maybe it won't. In the meantime, I've got it, for reference purposes. Now let's drink up, sweetheart. And if you ever doubt me again, ask me, instead of running away."

"Sometimes we're afraid of the answers, we who run away."

I lifted my glass. "To Cupid," I said.

"Who he?" she said.

"A baby-doll," I said.

Before we could get real comfy on Tony's champagne, it was four o'clock, lock-up time. Tony had not returned, his manager would close for him. We were the only customers left, aside from Linda and Bruce, and they were getting ready to go.

So were we. Linda and Bruce preceded us.

When we came out, it was teeming rain. The canopy of Royal House extended from doorway to curb, and the lights of the canopy hit our eyes, making a vague blurred periphery of the sheet-rain in the dimness beyond. Bruce and Linda were at the curb, Bruce saying, "You stay here, under the canopy. I'll get the car."

"Take us too," Suzy called from the doorway.

Then we heard the roar of the stepped-up motor, the three shots, and we saw the car tear past and round the corner. I ran after it, but it was no use, it was gone. I ran back. Suzy and Bruce were bent over Linda. "She's hurt bad," Bruce said. "We've got to get her to a hospital. Stay with her. I'll get the car."

TWENTY-SIX

THE YOUNG RESIDENT physician said: "Dr. John Harley is operating. He was here on an emergency. Ruptured appendix. As far as that goes, you're lucky. Harley's the best."

"How lucky are we with Miss Moreno?" I said.

He shrugged. "Critical. Touch and go. You said three shots were fired, didn't you?"

"Three shots," Bruce said. "We heard them distinctly."

"Well, only one of them hit. It tore through her lung, lodged in the spine. Terrific internal hemorrhaging. Maybe Harley can work a miracle. Personally, I doubt it."

Suzy sobbed.

"Look," the young resident said, "I'm going to have to call the police. Any gunshot wound, it's a police matter."

He went away and we sat, numbly, waiting.

Once Bruce said, "I don't get it. I just don't understand." But mostly we said nothing. We sat, numbly, waiting.

The police arrived in the persons of Detective-sergeant Anderson and Detective-sergeant Wiley. I knew them both. They were Parker's people. Anderson was the talker. "Hi," he said when he saw me. "What happened?"

"Where's Louie?" I said.

"Home sleeping. He's entitled, isn't he?"

"Yeah," I said.

"What happened?"

I told him.

"I see," Anderson said. "So you and Miss Lyons were practically bystanders, right?"

"Right," I said.

"Stick around," he said. "Mr. Lawson."

"Yes?" Bruce said.

"You were with Miss Moreno?"

"Yes."

"Good friends?"

"Yes."

"Okay, I want to hear all about your evening, from beginning to end. I want to know everything you know about her, from beginning to end. Look, would you come into the resident's office with us? We can kind of spread out there, make our notes."

"Yes," Bruce said.

Anderson said, "Stick around," and he and Wiley and Lawson went downstairs to the resident's office. Suzy and I sat, numbly waiting, smoking, not talking. Then the resident came into the little waiting room with a small white-haired man. "This is Dr. Harley," he said.

"How do you do, sir?" I said. "How is she?"

His eyes were soft and kindly and tired and compassionate, but his voice was clipped and clear. "She is dying," he said. "I did whatever I could for her, but whatever I did was not enough. If you are friends of hers, I suggest you go and see her at once. She is in 509."

114

"How long, Doc?" I said.

"Five minutes, half an hour . . ." He shrugged.

"Doctor, whatever your bill is—"

"There is no charge," he said. "Now I suggest you go at once . . ."

The resident went with us to a small darkened room. There was one shaded light on a table and no other illumination. The room was filled with the sick-sweet odor of ether and I had to swallow hard to keep from being ill. Only Linda's head showed on the bed, tilted upward, the sheets tight to her chin. Her eyes were open but glazed and her breathing was shallow and rasping. A nurse was on the other side of the bed.

I went near and I bent to her. "Linda. Linda, can you hear me?"

She seemed to want to smile. "Peter," she whispered. "Suzy, good kid."

Suzy sobbed. Linda's eyes looked toward her, then the eyes closed. But the breathing continued, more softly now. We could see the rise and fall of the sheet over her.

"Linda," I said. "Linda!"

The eyes opened. Her tongue wet her lips.

"Do you know who did this? Do you know who shot you?"

"No." The eyes closed. There was no sound except the shallow breathing. But suddenly the head wrenched off the pillow. The eyes opened, glaring. "Freddie," she said. "Freddie . . . didn't . . . kill himself."

"Who killed him, Linda?"

"I . . . I don't know." She gasped. There was a gurgling sound in her throat. She whispered: "The note. The suicide note. He . . . he wrote it . . . while I was there . . . in the room." The eyes closed again, then opened, straining. "Not . . . not a suicide note." Then the eyes closed again.

I straightened up. The resident touched a finger to his temple. "Delirium," he said quietly.

"Maybe not," I said. "She may have some information, important information, about a death. May I press her?"

"You heard what Dr. Harley said."

I patted her cheek, gently. "Linda, Linda," I said.

Her body trembled as she tried to raise her head from the pillow. The eyes opened wide, and there was intelligence in them. Again the tongue protruded, wetting the lips. "He . . . he wrote it . . . like always . . . boasting he was not drunk . . . boasting memory." The head fell back into the pillow. "He . . . he wrote it . . . it was there on the desk . . . when I went out."

"Why didn't you tell us? Why didn't you tell us, Linda?"

The smile was ghastly on the bloodless lips. "Murder . . .

115

murder I would lose. The will . . . crazy Freddie's will. Murder . . . I would lose. Why should I tell? Why should I?"

She was silent for a long time now, her eyes closed. The resident took her hand out from beneath the sheet, held her wrist. "She's all but gone now . . ."

But she pulled her wrist away. She sat up, her eyes bright and staring. "Freddie," she said clearly. "Cockroach . . . boasting Freddie . . . memory . . . the cockroach . . . cockroach . . ."

"Delirium," the resident said.

Then she fell back.

Then the eyes rolled up.

Then the sheet remained still.

The resident took her wrist. Then he pulled the sheet from her and used his stethoscope. Then he took the stethoscope from his ears and let it hang around his neck. Then he pulled the sheet up, all the way, until it covered her head.

Detective-sergeant Anderson said, "Why the hell didn't you call me?"

"There wasn't time," I said.

"Did she have any idea who had popped her?"

"No. No idea."

"You asked her?"

"Definitely. She had no idea."

"Well, it ain't just a shooting now, it's homicide. I'm afraid I'll have to ask all of you to come downtown with me."

Downtown, Detective-lieutenant Morton was in charge. He was a wizened little guy, snappy and to the point, but until the statements were typed, and the histories taken, and all the questions asked, it was ten o'clock in the morning before we were released.

"What are you going to do?" I asked Lawson.

"I got work, dammit," he said. "How about you?"

"I'm a little more free-lance than you," I said. "I'm going to take a nap."

We took him to his car, waved him off, and grabbed a cab to my place. The rain had stopped and there was a glint of winter sun. We showered and freshened up. I said, "Cockroach," a few times, and Suzy said, "Poor Linda," a few times, and she made coffee and scrambled eggs and toast and set a real nice table, and I had just begun to dig into the eggs when I jumped as though I had been burnt. I upset her real nice table, coffee staining the tablecloth.

"Now what the hell!" Suzy said in aggrieved concern.

But I was climbing the walls, reaching to a top shelf in the bookcase.

"Please, please, please, what the hell?" Suzy chanted.

I brought down a book, blew dust from it, opened it, riffled for a page, and found it.

"Look when he gets literary," Suzy said.

"Quiet!" I got out my wallet and took out the suicide note. I gave her the note and I said, "You look at that while I read."

"What?"

"You look at that while I read." I lifted the book and began to read: "A suicide is a person who has considered his own case and decided that he is worthless and who acts as his own judge, jury and executioner and he probably knows better than anyone else whether there is justice in the verdict."

Suzy started to say, "So what . . . ?" but her eyes were still on the note. When she looked up, she saw that I had been reading from the book. "What the devil?" she said.

"This is a book," I said. "It's called *The Lives and Times Of Archy and Mehitabel,* by Don Marquis. It's a book that Freddie owns, that's part of a collection right there at the Lodge. Do you get it?"

"No."

"It's what Linda was trying to tell us. It's the thing I was telling you about that was bugging me in my unconscious. Remember Linda saying things like 'Freddie . . . his memory . . . the cockroach'?"

"Yes."

"Think, Suzy. Freddie and Linda were arguing. He was drunk. She accused him of being drunk. Now we're reconstructing. So Freddie, as always when he's loaded, wants to show her he's not loaded. So he makes a quote. Probably starts writing the quote and tells her drag down the book and you'll see that I'm right. Remember her saying: 'He . . . wrote it . . . when I was there . . . in the room'? Remember her saying: 'Boasting he was not drunk . . . boasting memory . . . it was there on the desk . . . when I went out.' "

"Yes, yes," Suzy said and ran to me, "Let's see that book."

I showed her. Over my shoulder she read it as it was written:

> *a suicide is a person who has considered his own case and decided that he is worthless and who acts as his own judge, jury and executioner and he probably knows better than anyone else whether there is justice in the verdict*

"Wow," Suzy said. "That's what she meant by cockroach. Archy the cockroach. Mehitabel the cat. Don Marquis' characters. Linda knew she was dying. She tried to square the

117

thing, to tell us that Freddie was murdered, *prove* to us that he was murdered."

"Christ, thanks," I said and I limply sank into the chair. "I'm glad you've got it. I'm glad you're with me."

"Yeah," Suzy said. "This wasn't a suicide note, and Linda knew it. It was a note he'd written before—not even a note— a quote. When it turned up in his pocket as a suicide note, Linda knew it was all a phony. She knew he'd been murdered. But if she opened up, she stood to lose $200,000. So she clammed. Tell you the truth, I don't blame her."

"Yes," I mused. "Even explains that indentation in the corner of the note—which could have been made by a fingernail."

"Go on, man," Suzy said. "You're cooking."

"Sometime between nine and twelve, somebody came into that study, somebody who wanted Freddie dead. Let's say Freddie was asleep, passed out. That somebody sees that note on the desk—a perfect suicide note in his own handwriting. The somebody uses the rope that was hanging on the wall. Let's discount fingerprints on the rope, they can easily be smudged, and it's a bad surface for fingerprints anyway. Properly knotted, the rope is placed around Freddie's neck, then flung over that square beam. Then Freddie is hoisted up, and the other end of the rope is attached to the hook at the fireplace. Freddie's dead—dead by hanging. Then the note, held in a corner by fingernails, is inserted into Freddie's pocket, and the overturned chair is placed beneath his feet. What have we got?"

"Suicide. Pure and simple." She sat down opposite me, lit a cigarette, smoked and lapped coffee. "Do you think it could have been Linda after all?"

"No."

"But why not? Suicide isn't murder. As a suicide—Freddie's clause in the will holds—as it did hold. She collects $200,000, she's rid of Freddie, and she's free to take on Bruce Lawson. She must have spent a fortune on that guy."

"No," I said.

"But why not?"

"You said it earlier tonight—this is my line of business. Linda was on her deathbed and she knew it. She said Freddie didn't kill himself. I asked her specifically: 'Who killed him, Linda?' She answered specifically: 'I don't know.' People just don't lie in those circumstances, plus she worked so damned hard to get it through to us just how it was done. No. Linda didn't kill him. No."

"Bruce Lawson?" Suzy said.

I fumbled with the eggs. "That's the guy with the *least* motive."

118

"But, wow, did he gain!"

"He wouldn't kill on the off-chance that Linda would start supporting him."

"No, I don't suppose he would."

I tasted the eggs. They were still warm. I ate, sipped coffee. "I wonder how much she spent on him," I said.

"We can easily find that out."

"Yeah?" I said. "How?"

"Cameron Shipworth," she said.

"And who the hell is Cameron Shipworth?"

"Her business manager. Mine too."

"Business manager? Real classy."

"When you get up a little bit in the brackets, in our racket, you need a business manager."

I put my fork down. "Where's he located?"

"15 Wall Street."

"Let's go down to see him."

"What for?"

"I don't know," I said. "Financial tangles sometimes untangle into motives for murder. Business manager. Some class. Let's go, kid."

"Not until you finish eating."

"Yes, ma'am," I said.

Dutifully, I finished eating.

TWENTY-SEVEN

CAMERON SHIPWORTH, on the twentieth floor of 15 Wall Street, was tall, narrow and imposing, with shrewd eyes and a high-pitched voice. Suzy introduced me and I said with as much portent as I could summon, "Linda Moreno."

"Dreadful, dreadful," quoth Cameron Shipworth.

"I am working in conjunction with Lieutenant Morton on her untimely decease and all assistance on your part will be appreciated."

Shipworth looked to Suzy and Suzy nodded sagely.

"I'll be glad to help howsoever I can, sir," Shipworth said, "but I'm afraid that will be very little."

"Thank you, sir," I said. "Now did Miss Moreno leave a will?"

"I'm not her lawyer, but I'm certain she didn't."

"How so, sir?"

"Because I recommended that several times, and she flatly refused to listen. You know actresses—superstitious. She simply refused to think of anything that might have to do with her death. She said that the making of wills was for old people, and that when she was old she would make one. If I might stray for a moment—Miss Lyons has made no will either."

"Uh huh," Suzy said and wrinkled her nose and looked shame-faced.

"Could you give me a general picture of her financial set-up," I said.

"Yes, of course. You see, actresses—and actors—are notoriously bad business people, which is why they need . . . er . . . people like me. Miss Moreno as star of *Flesh and Fury* received seven hundred and fifty dollars a week, which was augmented by occasional, and very well paying TV appearances. All monies were paid directly to me, and I doled out payments to her. I had her on a pretty strict schedule. One hundred and fifty dollars a week."

"No more?" I said.

"All the rest I invested—in a judicious selection of bonds, and in an annuity." He smiled sadly. "There was no need for more than a hundred and fifty dollars a week, not with Mr. Flanders as her . . . er . . . patron."

"And what happened after Mr. Flanders died?"

"Miss Moreno was by then—how shall I say it—broken in. She continued upon the same stipend. We hoped that within a very few years that stipend would be very much increased, since the deposit of the two hundred thousand dollars—after taxes—in one lump into her annuity."

"What two hundred thousand dollars?"

"Don't you know that Mr. Flanders' will—"

"You mean she turned that money over to you, all of it?"

"Of course. Every blessed penny."

"Well, did she have any other money?"

"She had—"

"I mean money that she could spend, real money, that she might be spending right now."

"No, sir. She had a thousand dollars in a savings account, but she wasn't spending that. The book is right here with me."

Abruptly I stood up. "Thank you, Mr. Shipworth."

"Not at all, sir. If there is anything else—"

"Thank you very much," I said and grabbed Suzy.

Downstairs, I practically dragged her to a saloon.

"What's with you?" she said gasping at the Scotch and soda in front of her.

"We have to revise our thinking. Where else, but a saloon?"

"What thinking? Open up, lover. I'm thick."

I tried to imitate Shipworth's high-pitched voice. "You see, my dear, I'm experiencing a revolution in my thought processes."

"Well, revolutionize me too, will you, kid?"

120

"Bruce Lawson. Where'd he get all that new finery if Linda didn't have any real dough to spend?"

"Oh, brother, am I *thick.*" She grinned. "You two up there, prattling away about finances in that phony language, I wasn't really listening, I was kind of dreaming . . ."

"Have you been up to his new place?"

"It's gorgeous."

"What's the address?"

"East 79th Street. But where'd he suddenly get it all from? Gorgeous apartment, classy duds, a brand new car, squiring Linda all over town . . ."

"Quiet," I said.

"What?" she said.

"Maybe the wrong party got hit."

"*What?*" she said.

"Bruce and Linda, they were standing together, there under that canopy. It was dark, fuzzy, rainy, and the shots came from a moving car. Three shots. Two missed. One hit. That one hit Linda. Suppose that bullet hit the wrong one. *Suppose those bullets were meant for Bruce Lawson.*"

"But why?"

"Sure," I said almost to myself. "He was accumulating lots of dough and not from Linda. He's a criminal investigator. Criminal investigators have lots of special knowledge. Could be that Brucie-boy added other knowledge to this special knowledge and made it pay off. Come on, sister. Up."

"Up?"

"Up and away."

First stop was my office where I slipped on a shoulder holster and slipped a pistol into the holster.

"What's that for?" Suzy said.

"In case of emergency."

"You expecting emergency?" she said.

"We're in emergency right now," I said. "About Lawson. Remember he said he had work to do today."

"Yes, that's right, he did."

"You know his home phone number?"

"Yes."

"Call him."

She called. There was no answer.

Then I called—Zangwill Manchester.

"Zang?" I said. "Chambers."

"Hi, Peep," he said.

"You owe me a favor," I said.

"Sure, but a guy's got to make a living," he bleated.

"Stop kidding," I said. "The favor is that I want you to move at once, it's an emergency. Money, you'll be paid—

an extra yard. Three hundred. And you don't have to worry about crossing this threshold. No bankers involved here. Strictly a crumb. I'm protecting you, all the way."

"Where do you want me, Peep?"

"Two East 79th."

"When?"

"Right now."

"I just left," he said and hung up.

We got there in a hurry, but Zang was already there with his little black bag, waiting. "I must say," he said, ogling Suzy, "this is much prettier company than last time."

"You'll get me into trouble," I said, "unless you tell her it was a man last time."

"It was a man last time," he said.

Two East 79th Street was proud, old, immaculate, Gothic, and distinguished. In the marble lobby I pushed the Lawson button. There was no answer. Zang performed his feat upon the door, and we entered an inner marble lobby, and then a silent mirrored self-service elevator.

"What floor?" I asked Suzy.

"Six. 6C."

I pushed for six.

"This building must be fifty years old," Zang said, "but it's beautiful. When they keep them beautiful, they stay beautiful."

Upstairs he opened 6C and we went visiting.

"Beautiful," Zang said. "Can I go now?"

"Sit down," I said. "I've got a hunch there'll be more work. I told you there's nothing to worry about. The guy's a crumb."

"You ought to know," he said. I didn't know how to take that so I let it pass.

There were three spacious airy high-ceilinged rooms—drawing room, bedroom and kitchen—all beautiful and exquisitely furnished. "Must have cost him twenty thousand bucks to set this joint up," I said. "Maybe more, since it was done in a hurry."

"She's beautiful," Zang said, wistfully gazing upon Suzy who had removed her coat.

"Thank you," Suzy said shyly.

"Just sit and look at her," I said. "I'll be with you shortly."

I worked the place over, inch by inch, starting with the drawing room. In the bedroom closet, behind heaps of hanging clothes, I found what I had hoped for. Set into the rear wall of the closet was a large old-fashioned safe. These wall safes were not unusual in these old houses. Perhaps that

122

was why Lawson had selected an old house to move into. "Zang!" I yelled.

He came, with Suzy.

"What's this?" I said and pointed.

"A garbage can," he scoffed. "The old-timers always had them built in, like today they got air-conditioning."

"Can you open it?"

"Are you kidding?" he said. "One thing I'll say for them, though. They're still fire-proof."

"Looks real rugged."

"Out of my way, professor," Zang said, and in five minutes the heavy steel door swung open. "Crazy," Zang said as he peered in.

I removed the contents of the safe: a rope, a camera, and two large manilla envelopes.

"Crazy," Zang said as I bore my trophies to the drawing room.

"Like a fox," I said.

I opened the envelopes. One contained forty glistening photographs; the other, the forty negatives of the same photographs. I spread them on the desk and studied them. Suzy looked once, and went away and sat down. Zang looked with me. "Crazy," he said.

There were pictures of Freddie Flanders, eyes popped, hanging by his neck. They were close shots, far shots, angle shots. There were shots of the rope, shots of the room, long shots, close shots: a complete portfolio. "Can I have one of your magnifying glasses, Zangie, my lad?" I said.

"My pleasure," Zang said. "What kind of a crumb *is* this crumb?"

"A private investigator."

"Oh, one of them crumbs," Zang said, and grinned, and brought me the glass.

I used it to study the rope, and the photographs, and I said, "Sure enough. Brucie-boy's just as smart as I thought he was."

And then Brucie-boy himself came home.

There was the rasp of the key in the lock and there he was. He strode into the drawing room, took a quick look, and roared: "What the hell goes?"

"It's all over now, Brucie-boy," I said.

He rushed at me and it was a rush I had been waiting for since I'd met him. He swung, I ducked, and I belted him. It caught him on the cheek, but Brucie-boy was strong. He brushed it off and came again. He got a left that went to the wrist in his gut. Brucie-boy winced, he was soft in the gut. So he got two more like that, each bringing a grunt. I let him unbend because I was enjoying myself. He came again and this time he got the right full swing to the gut, and tears sprang to his eyes. He bent double, holding his hands to his stomach, and moaning. So now I wound up, and pitched one underhand, direct to the jaw. Brucie-boy's feet left the floor—all of Brucie-boy left the floor—and Brucie-boy returned to the floor with a thud. He lay on his back, whimpering.

"Crazy," Zang said.

Brucie-boy was strong. He sat up. He did not get up. He *sat* up.

"More?" I inquired.

"No more," he said.

"Brucie-boy," I said, "here, in your possession, are a group of items which are unequivocal evidence of murder, the murder of Freddie Flanders."

"I had nothing to do with his murder," he said from the floor.

"Keep sitting where you are," I said. "Whether you're held for murder, or as an accomplice, or merely for extortion depends, I would say, on your attitude right now. So just take it easy, huh?" I took my gun from its holster and gave it to Zang.

"Thank you," Zang said sweetly. "What do I do with this?"

"You point it at the crumb," I said. "Any undue activity on the crumb's part, you shoot him, as a favor to me. I guarantee you protection on this. Matter of fact, it would earn you a citation."

"Citations I need," Zang said, "like you need a hole in the head. However, I would be happy to shoot your friend, I mean as a favor to you."

"Did you hear him?" I asked of Bruce.

"I heard him," Bruce said.

"He means it," I said.

"Oh, yes, of course I do," Zang said mildly.

"You didn't kill him?" I said.

"No," Bruce said.

"Bruce," I said, "a question. I think I know the answer, but this question. How come all this stuff is here in the wall safe? Don't you have a vault?"

"Yes, I have."

"Then why here?"

"I thought about it, thought hard. I wanted to prevent —what actually happened here. I felt that if anybody got wind of it, got close—then they'd tie up my vault, and I was cooked. With the stuff here, the moment I smelled something wrong—I could get here first and destroy the whole works. Either way was risky. I figured this for less risky."

124

"Thanks. So I thought. You're playing ball, Brucie. I appreciate it."

"I know when I'm licked," he said. "You don't even need the man with the gun."

"He's enjoying himself," I said.

"I am," Zang said.

"You don't want to spoil a man's fun," I said.

"Now just a minute," Suzy said. "I don't understand what's going on here. Evidence of murder? What evidence of murder? The rope, the pictures, the camera—what evidence of murder? What are you two talking about?"

"Mostly," I said, "we're talking about the rope and the fibres of the rope."

"Rope? Fibres?" Suzy looked utterly bewildered.

"When there's a hanging like this," I said, "the police can tell whether it's murder or suicide. So can trained investigators, like Bruce or myself."

"You learn something new every day," Zang said.

"But how?" Suzy said.

"From the fibres of the rope," I said.

"But how?" Suzy said.

"All right, listen. A guy's going to hang himself, what does he do? First he attaches one end of the rope to something. In this case it would have been the hook at the fireplace. Then the person flings the rope over a support. In this case one of the square beams beneath the ceiling. Then the person would stand on a chair or something, put the noose around his neck, and kick the chair away. Got it so far?"

"Yes."

"His weight pulls the rope slightly, the noose tightens, and he chokes to death. A close examination of the fibres of the rope, especially near the support—in this case the wooden beam—corroborates this, or refutes it."

"But how? What would the fibres show?"

"The weight of the body would pull on the rope. Yes?"

"Yes."

"Thus the fibres of the rope, near the beam, on the side attached to the body, would all point upward. The fibres on the other side of the beam, away from the body, would all point downward. This is because the weight of the body pulled that rope. Understand?"

"Yes, I think so . . ."

I unbuckled my belt and pulled it from my pants. "Come here," I said, "I'll show you." I slung the belt over the arm of one of the wooden chairs in the room. "Pretend," I said, "that the buckle is the body." I held the belt tight to the arm of the chair and slowly pulled the buckle side downward. "See what I mean?" I said. "As I pull on the buckle side—here where the belt moves along the arms of the chair—the fibres would go upward. Understand?"

"Yes. Yes, I do."

"That," I said, "would tend to prove suicide. But the opposite situation would clearly show—murder! Thus, a murderer tosses a rope across a beam. He puts the noose around a neck. He hauls the body up, to simulate suicide, and attaches the other end to the hook. What happens to the fibres then? Exactly the reverse! Observation of the fibres close to the beam would disclose *that they all point upward on that section of the rope pulled by the murderer —and downward on that section of the rope from which the body is hanging.*"

"I see. I understand."

"Now come here and take a look at this rope. It's an old one, you hardly need the magnifying glass. See where the indentations of the square beam are? Now look at the fibres on this side, away from the noose. *All going upward.* And on the side of the noose? *Downward.* An experienced eye would instantly know it was murder, not suicide. If you look at the closeups of the photographs with this magnifying glass, you'll see exactly the same. Murder, not suicide."

"You learn something new every day," Zang said.

"And now Brucie-boy," I said, "if you please . . ."

TWENTY-EIGHT

Twenty minutes later, in the downstairs living room of the house on Sixty-second Street, Ethel Flanders, confronted by all the evidence, said in a hushed voice that was more terrifying than a scream:

"Yes, I killed him. I'm glad it's over."

"Would you tell us, please?" I said.

She was leaning back in a corner of a sofa. Her face was grey. Her hands were limp in her lap. "When the house was quiet, I decided to go down there. It had been bad, horrible, and I wanted it settled once and for all. Bringing that woman there, I was ashamed, not only for myself, for Sara." Tears came from her eyes, slow tears. She did not seem to feel them. She raised no hand to wipe them. "Sara was asleep. I took a flashlight from my drawer and went down there. He was vicious, absolutely vicious. He called me vile names, told me I was worse than the woman he had brought there. Suddenly it came to climax, all my shameful years with him, came to climax. I wanted to kill

126

him, to end it, if only there was a way. And just then, he sighed and passed out, drunk and unconscious. And that's when I saw the note on the desk, and that's when I knew there was a way."

"Now you," I said to Bruce Lawson.

"I couldn't sleep. I was going down for a hot chocolate. When I got to the head of the stairs, I saw her come out of the study, shooting the beam of the flashlight ahead of her. I figured something was cockeyed, so I stepped back into the shadows, waited till she got to her room, then went down there. He was dead."

"Then what?"

"Did what you'd expect. Examined the rope. No question she'd killed him."

"Then?"

"I was mixed with rich people, millionaires. I figured maybe an angle would work itself out. I just went back to my room and waited."

"And at twelve o'clock when the screaming started . . . ?"

"I came down with the rest. I played along. When we found that the phones were dead, I did the photo bit, still hoping for an angle. Then when we found the bridge down, I knew I had an angle, because now I had time. During the night, I took him down, then I took the rope, camera and film to the Reynolds' House. I found a metal container in the basement. I put the stuff into that, and buried it in the snow in the backyard."

"And picked it up when you went for Nick at the hospital."

"Yes. After the will was probated and the money was paid, I came to Mrs. Flanders with my story. Told her I had seen her, told her about the evidence I had, explained that to her, asked her for fifty thousand dollars, and got it."

"He's a liar," she said. "He didn't leave me alone."

I began to dial Police Headquarters.

"He didn't leave me alone," she said. Behind the tears, her eyes were wide and clean, and as though purified by torture, as innocent as a child's. "I paid him what he asked, but he wanted more. He wanted a hundred thousand dollars now. And he wanted fifty thousand dollars a year, every year. It wasn't the money. I had wanted it ended—after twenty-five years—I had wanted it ended, and now it was not ended, it was a trap again, and I had so wanted to be free. I was confused, crazy. It was all so monstrous, unreal. I waited in the car outside Royal House, I waited in the rain, waited with a gun, waited because I wanted to be free. And then, today, from the newspapers, I learned that Linda was dead, that I had killed Linda, that he was still alive, and I wanted to tell, but I was afraid, and I'm

glad you are here, glad it's over, but I wanted to be free,
oh please try to understand, I so wanted, at long last, to be
free, free, free . . ."

She toppled from the sofa, in a dead faint, as the voice
on the phone chirped, "Yes? Police Headquarters. This is
Police Headquarters. Yes? What is it? Hello? Hello . . ."

www.ingramcontent.com/pod-product-compliance
Lightning Source LLC
Chambersburg PA
CBHW010643100726
47900CB00011B/2944